PECULIAR RELATIONSHIPS

A fictional novel that describes the evolving relationships between black women and white women from slavery to current day

To Linda,
The Struggle Continues!
P+L
G. Ragsn

by Gwen Ragsdale

Order this book online at www.trafford.com
or email orders@trafford.com

Most Trafford titles are also available at major online book retailers.

Printed in the United States of America.

ISBN: 978-1-4907-3886-4 (sc)
ISBN: 978-1-4907-3885-7 (hc)
ISBN: 978-1-4907-3884-0 (e)

Library of Congress Control Number: 2014910273

Trafford rev. 06/18/2014

 www.trafford.com

North America & international
toll-free: 1 888 232 4444 (USA & Canada)
fax: 812 355 4082

I dedicate this book to my Sister Friends. Some of you were with me for a season, others for a reason but you will always have a special place in my heart. Those who left way too soon, I pray we get to reconnect in a better place. As for my close circle of ride or die sister friends, and you know who you are; I can't thank you enough for your:

- ➢ Love
- ➢ Prayers
- ➢ Advice
- ➢ Encouragement
- ➢ Support

For saying when I needed it; "Really Raggs?"
I love you more than you'll ever know. Thank you for always being there when I needed you, even when I didn't think I did.
You are truly the "Wind Beneath My Wings"

TABLE OF CONTENTS

CHAPTER I

CHAPTER II

CHAPTER III

CHAPTER IV

CHAPTER V

CHAPTER VI

EPILOGUE

CHAPTER 1

Charlottesville, Virginia, 1855

MATTIE, MISS LILLIE, AND MISS BLUE EYES

Mattie my name; I'se so tide, seem lak I been working from "sunup to sunup." I never get no rest. Miss Lillie keeps barking orders at me "Do dis, do dat!" Sometime when she send me to do yet anudder thing, I hurry and do it, so I can sneak away fo' a little rest. One day I was sleeping down by the creek bed when, the overseer come up on me; he grabbed me up so fast I can't tell if I'se dreaming or if it real! I find out soon enuff, when he slapped me cross the face. He dragged me by my ear back to the Big House. Where Miss Lillie beat me with a stick til' it broke. The mo" I cried for mercy, the mo" she hit me. She a mean, hateful white woman; even worse when she drinks, which she often do. Ever since her husband died, she been wallowing in pity and growing meaner by the day. She ain't got much money, but she make out like she do. Her house is run-down and needs patching and painting. Her crops wilting, her animals skinny, and her slaves don't look much better. We has little to eat, raggedy clothes, and a shanty lean-to that leaks when it rains; we suffers bad! I got a pitiful life; been beat and treated poorly fo" most of it. I give birth to seven children: four sons and three daughters. Four of 'em died befo" age five; two was torn from my breast and sold soon after birth. Only child I got left is my daughter Precious. At nine, she my longest living child, fars I know anyhow. Female slaves don't have no say about who or how many chilun they get to keep. We never know when we might be set upon; no matter yo" age, whether you be eight or eighty.. Any man, white or colored, can take you any given time and ain't nuttin' you can do 'bout it. Which why, my chillun come out so many different colors; some white as snow, others black as coal, and erything in between. Slave women who lives in the Big House mo" apt to be taken by white men, cuz they round 'em mo'. Happened to me and seen it happen to many udder slave women time and time agin.

I'se blessed I got to keep my daughter Precious; she such a sweet child. Dat's why I name her Precious and glad white folks ain't change it. She was born rat here on this sorry plantation and been wit me ever since she come in the world. We share this sad life together; she loves me and I love her more than anything; without her, I won't have no reason to live. Every night befo' I lay my head down, I pray to God my Precious will someday have a better life then mine, do all I can to keep her safe. I keep her with me all the time, try not to let her out my sight, when I can help it. It's a miracle I been able to keep her safe all dese years. I don't trust nobody with my child, cuz I know what can happen to a slave girl. Jes the udder day, I hear 'bout a slave mother and her eight-year-old daughter who was both beat and taken by a group of white men. Hard to make sense of men who would do dat to a mere child, and they call us animals. Awful things happen to slaves every day; you jes get used to it.

Sometime they make us watch when a slave gets whipped to teach us all a lesson. I seen plenty whippings, beatings, and hangings in my lifetime, and when it ain't happening to you you go 'bout your bizness thankful it ain't.

2

But if 'yo time ever come or you be forced to watch yo loved ones git beat; the pain be so much worse. Not from the lashing alone, but knowing you can't even help yoself, much less nobody else. Being a slave is a sad and terrible life, full of endless pain and misery with no end in sight.

One day, me and Precious was in the kitchen; I was teaching her how to cook, clean, and do things round the house, and she was doing real good too. That is, til' Miss Lillie come in screaming 'bout her table not being set right. I tried to tell her my girl just learning and dat I'll fix it rat away, but she ain't wanna hear it she was set on beating my child. She picked up the cool end of a burning piece of wood out the fireplace and reached to hit Precious cross her head, but I put my arm in the way. Miss Lillie came cross my forearm with dat burning log so hard I heard it crack, than my sleeve caught fire. I screamed out in pain and ran to a bucket of water sitting in the corner; at the same time, I pushed Precious out the door and told her to run. I was in so much pain I could barely stand it, but I took it cuz dat blow woulda surely killed my child. Don't know how many mo" Miss Lillie's beatings I can take, but I caint chance doing nuttin' dat might force me and Precious apart. Don't know what I'd do if we was, she all I got and I all she got. Took some time fo' my arm to heal and when it did it I was left with a lasting crook in it and a terrible burn scar. I could tell the sight of my arm made Miss Lillie uneasy, so I often keep my sleeve rolled up so she always git to see what she did to me. She threaten to break my udder arm, but I gave her a look dat let her know she would have a fight on her hands this time. I'se tired of her beatings and ain't gonna take no mo'.

After church on Sundays, Miss Lillie have teas for her lady friends. They far more fancy than her, but she go out her way to make like she is, but you could tell they know she ain't. One of the white ladies keeps smiling at me; I don't look back, but when she turns her glance, I take a quick look at her. She was beautiful; she had pure white skin, long black hair, and the bluest eyes I ever seed befo'. I don't know her name, but to myself, I call her Miss Blue Eyes. Seems like she wanna say sumptin' to me, but I don't look her in the eye, cuz dat ain't 'llowed. Cept for Miss Lillie, I ain't never speak wid no other white woman befo', so I keep my head down. I hear tell she's the new mistress at the nearby Wilson Plantation and dat they treat they slaves real good there. I dream 'bout being sold to her; I'd take real good care of her and her family, wouldn't mine being her slave at all. Anudder Sunday I was serving the white tea ladies when Miss Blue Eyes asked me right in front of all of 'em, "Mattie, what happened to your arm?" I ack like I ain't hear her and jes keep on pouring the tea. In my head I thinking; she called me by my name, not girl or nigger, but then, I wonder why she asked me dat in the first place. Then I got up my nerve and said; "You needs to ask Miss Lillie, ma'am?"

All the white ladies spin they heads round and looked straight at Miss Lillie, but she quickly looked away; she ain't say a word. I turned and hurried out the room. I could tell these fancy ladies don't wanna be round no foolishness, and they know Miss Lillie full of foolishness. I was still waiting on the white tea ladies, and I see Miss Lillie over in the corner trying to ack bigger then she is, so I sneak anudder look at pretty Miss Blue Eyes. I ain't want her to catch me, so I don't lift my head and just looked out the side of my eye. I was surprised to see her looking right back at me, and when her blue eyes met my brown eyes, my spirit was warmed by her kind and caring face. The white ladies began gathering up they belongings to leave, when Miss Blue Eyes dropped her glove, so I ran over and picked it up. When I hand it up to her, she let her fingers touch my arm. I 'tempted to pull away, but she held on to me and smiled. I was skeered and happy all at the same time. I won't never round no white woman lak her befo"; she so warm and friendly and treats me lak I as human as she is. Miss Blue Eyes was 'bout to leave when I hear her ask Miss Lillie if she would hire me out.

My heart almost leaped out my chest when I heard her say dat, but I jest keep clearing the table. Right away, Miss Lillie said *no*, but Miss Blue Eyes kept pressing her.

"Lillie, you have plenty of help around here. I could use Mattie to train my staff. Both she and her daughter would be quite helpful to me, I will pay you handsomely."

Soon as she mention money, Miss Lillie's eyes lit up. Miss Blue Eyes know she needs money bad.

They talked for what seemed lak a awful long time, they musta struck up a deal, cuz befo' I knowed it, me and Precious was packed up in the back of Miss Blue Eyes' wagon and headed for what I believed would be a better life for us both.

A Brand New Beginning

When we arrived at Miss Blue Eyes' plantation, it was everything I dreamed 'bout and more. The Wilson Plantation was clean and well kept. They had acres of tall cotton, white as snow, big tobacco plants, and the corn looked like it was busting out the stalks. The Big House was the biggest I ever seed. It had a porch dat wrapped clear round the house with white rocking chairs. The sun bounced off bright, clean windows with pretty blue shutters. They had a bountiful vegetable garden out back with big red, plump tomatoes, greens, okra, carrots, taters, and more. *Umm, umm, umm;* seems the Lawd heard my prayers after all. It's lak I died and went to heaven and me and Precious gonna walk round heaven all day. "Thank you, Jesus!"

Miss Blue Eyes took me to meet her husband; his name is Massa William Wilson. He's a tall, slender, sandy-haired, handsome-looking man. He was born and raised rat here in Charlottesville; he's a lawyer and a Virginia senator and comes from a wealthy family. His daddy was a 'spectable judge; he passed away a few years ago and his mother just passed too, so he come back home to run his family farm. He and Miss Blue Eyes make a striking-looking couple. She come from Philadelphia, Pennsylvania, where they met and went to school. She much mo' refined and talk mo' proper then the udder white women round here, 'special Miss Lillie. You can always tell the wealth of a plantation owner by how well his plantation is kept and how his slaves look and live. These slaves look well fed; they all dressed well and seem in high spirits. Many of 'em got on shoes; good ones. I ain't never had no good shoes jes po' fitting hand-me-downs. Precious ain't never have none at all; I wonder if she even know how to walk in shoes guess she can learn though. I went down to slave row where I saw rows of clean, stone cabins. Nuttin' lak the stinking, shanty house, with dirt floors dat turned to mud when it rained, we lived in at Miss Lillie's awful place. It was corn harvest time, and the slaves "vited me and Precious to join 'em in a *shuck and jive.* As we shucked the corn, we danced and sang around a huge bonfire; I never had so much fun. For the first time in my life, I was happy and so was Precious; never seen her smile so broad. If we has to be slaves, then this the place we need to be and gonna stay. I can't help but wonder if slavery can be this good what must freedom be lak?

Me and Precious live in the Big House in a room just off the kitchen. I can see why she needs my help; they already got a house mammy, but she real old and moves slow. They tell me she raised Massa Wilson which 'splain why he keep her 'round. Some white folks often love they mammies mo' den they own mamas and when the mammies git too old to work they keep 'em anyhow and let 'em live out the rest they lives in peace. But you could tell this mammy's best days behind her, she don't seem to mind my help at all, so I went right to work. They got a good number of house slaves, but none of 'em know how to run a household. Miss Blue Eyes let 'em know I'se the new house Mammy; they took it in stride and looked to me to tell 'em what to do and how to do it. It won't long befo' things start shaping up round the Wilson household.

Most plantations have white overseers, and well-to-do ones have many of 'em. Most times they po' white men, but the Wilson plantation ain't got no overseers at all; they jes got two colored slave drivers. They call whites overseers and coloreds slave drivers, but they both do the same tend to slaves.

Nigger slave drivers can be jes as mean and ill-tempered as white overseers and been known to lash slaves with the same quickness. Sometime, they even meaner, to show massas they can handle niggers too. Dese colored slave drivers is twin brothers; they both big, strong, strapping, good-looking boys. One is dark and one is light. The dark one got brown eyes and the light one got green eyes, but they both got the same face and even sound alike too. I smiled at 'em, they the oddest pair of twin brothers I ever seen befo'. They names is Dori and Gray. Dori, the dark one, smiles a lot and do most the talking; Gray, quiet and kinda brooding; he don't say much at all. Dori told me Massa Wilson's daddy, Judge Wilson, bought dem as a gift for his eighth birthday to be his playmates, cuz he an only child. Said they was eight too, dat was twenty years ago, and they been with him ever since. The brothers educated and traveled all round the country and abroad with Massa Wilson. The three of 'em is real close, said they do anything for Massa Wilson and he would do the same fo' them. I hear of two peas in a pod befo', but they mo' like three peas in the pod. *Tee hee!*

As time went on, I starts to feel rat at home; this place so much better than where we come from. Massa Wilson be gone much of the time doing his lawyer bizness, and leaves Miss Blue Eyes to run the plantation with the help of the trusted brothers and other loyal slaves. She keep asking me what I think 'bout different things but I ain't always sho' what to say. I wanna help her much as I can but I don't know but so much, after all I'se just a slave. Looks lak the Wilson slaves oversee theyselves, for the most part. The brothers only harsh on slaves who don't carry they workload or act out, but most times, these slaves seem to do as they told. If a slave git outta line, udder slaves steps up and straighten 'em out rat away. Ain't no slave in his right mind willing to lose what little freedom they got, so the slaves mind they p's and q's. They sho' do things different round the Wilson Plantation, but it seem to work for 'em. Sumptin else strange; slaves keep coming up missing, sometime whole families, but then they quickly buy new ones dat's real strange. This go on agin and agin, but when I ask 'bout a slave I ain't seen in a while, the brothers say they don't know who I be asking 'bout or tell me they was sold off. But dat makes me wonder even more, cuz I never see none of 'em leave. *Hmmm?*

Strange Goin's-on

What dese boys telling me don't make no sense; no sense at all! Why in heaven's name do they keep buying new slaves when they can keep the ones they already got? Anudder strange thing goes on round here at night. Miss Blue Eyes tell me to make sho" the lantern in the front yard is always lit even through the night, when I ask her why, she got real terse wit me and said, "Because I said so!" The last thing I wanna do is make Miss Blue Eyes cross with me; she the best owner I ever had, so from here on out, I'm gonna keep my mouff shut and just do as I'se told. She had me make up satchels of vittles and leave out on the back porch, saying they was for the slaves going to auction. Dat don't make no sense to me, but I don't ask no questions. Most times, when slaves merely hear the word auction they git real fearful, special the females. Right away, they start hollering and screaming; 'fraid they gonna be sold or have they chillun sold away from 'em. Dat's a scary time fo' all slaves; I know the last thing they be thinking 'bout is eating but I don't say a word. Dese slaves keep calm, lak they sneaking away or sumptin.' But I never see none of 'em leave seem lak they vanish into thin air. Everybody ack lak what's going on is normal as day turns to night, but it ain;t. There always lots of commotion at night too; not a lotta noise, jest lots of moving 'bout. Dese some strange goin's on.

My mind gits the best of me, I can't wonder no mo' I need to find out what's going on, so one night, I sneaked down to the slave quarters, hid in the woods, and jest sat by and watched. I saw a number of wagons being loaded up with slaves; they all had a satchel of food I packed earlier. But when they git in the wagon, they have 'em lay down then, they cover 'em over and put bales of cotton on top of 'em. *What for?* I wonder. If they going to auction, why they need to hide 'em? I got more questions than I do answers. Then I hear a voice come from behind me "What you doing down here?"

I turned round and saw Gray, one of the twins. He gently led me back to the Big House and told me to go wait in the parlor for the Missus. This same thing happened to me befo', when I was with Miss Lillie, and she almost to beat me to deaf. I'se 'fraid the same thing gonna happen to me again. Is Miss Blue Eyes gonna beat me too? I'se so skeered my knees shaking.

Then the door opened, and both Miss Blue Eyes followed by Massa Wilson walked in. He sat down behind his desk and she stood next to him. They both just stared at me then Miss Blue Eyes asked me "Mattie, why were you sneaking around the slave quarters"?

I wannna say but I'se so skeered the words won't come out ma mouff. I looked over at Massa Wilson he ain't say a word, just keep looking at me real stern. Both him and Miss Blue Eyes been nuttin' but kind to me; I feel so bad. I broke down crying, and befo" I could help myself, I shouted out, "Massa Wilson, they stealing yo' slaves!"

He looked at me for a long time. Then he said, "Who's stealing my slaves, Mattie?"

"I don't know for sho', suh, but I believe it's the brothers." Then I opened up like a flood gate and began gushing out erything I seen. "Massa, they stealing yo' slaves, bringing in new ones and hoping you can't tell the difference, but I can." "Massa, for the life of me, I can't understand how those boys can do this to you, after you treat 'em so good and keep 'em round so long? It ain't right what they doing to you, Massa. It just ain't right! They work under the cover of night, bring in new slaves, and steal the old ones. What they doing don't make no sense, but they doing it just the same. I'se so sorry to have to tell you all this, Massa, but you can't trust them nigger boys. They not to be trusted, I tell you." I stopped just long enough to catch my breath, than started rat up again. "Massa, you and Missus the best owners I ever had; I cain't sit back and let this go on no longer.

You gotta do sumptin', Massa. It ain't right, jes ain't right what they doing." I was crying so hard I could barely breathe, but I keep on. I tell 'em 'bout the slaves I seen laid down in wagons and covered with bales of cotton.

Miss Blue Eyes starts coming toward me; I braced myself for the blows I was 'specting to rain down on me at any time. But she put her arm round me and said "Settle down, Mattie. It's not what you think." She keeps patting my back. "We can explain everything."

But befo' she could, Massa Wilson asked me, "Mattie, do you believe in God?"

I wiped my face and tried to calm maself down befo' I answered him, *sniff.* "Yes suh, I do

"We also believe in God and slavery is not God's doing. It's man's doing, namely the white man, that's why we became abolitionists." *"A-bo-lish-niss,* what dat, suh?"

"We help slaves escape to freedom.""You do?""Yes, we do. We fervently believe that slavery is wrong. It's against everything we stand for, including our religion. As Quakers we believe that all people are equal in the eyes of God, no matter their color or status in life. This is very serious, it's important you understand what we're doing. We could lose our plantation, be thrown in jail, even lose our lives, there's no telling what might happen, because what we're doing is against the law."

Miss Blue Eyes spoke up "Mattie, I saw how badly Miss Lillie was treating you. That's why I conjured up a way to get you and Precious away from her. No one deserved to be treated the way she treated you. We're all God's children, white and colored alike. We want to free you and Precious and as many other slaves as we possibly can. I've made her several generous offers but she has rejected every one of them; telling me she just wants to hire you out and continues to raise her cost, which we eagerly pay every time. We need to be very careful, if she or anyone else finds out what we're doing not only will we be in peril, but many others involved in similar operations like ours will be as well."

Massa turned my head to face him. "Mattie listen to me; myself and a few other members of the Virginia Assembly have issued a petition calling for the manumission of slavery meaning we want to free all the slaves, but we don't have enough votes at this time. We're trying to change the minds of other lawmakers, but it's going to take some time. We're close, but we're not there yet. Until then, we can't stand by and do nothing to help these powerless souls."

"Mattie, we need your help. Can we trust you to keep our secret?" Miss Blue Eyes added "From the moment I laid eyes on you, Mattie, I believed we could trust you. Will you help us?"

My head was dizzy trying to keep up with all they was telling me. Without even thinking, I said "Course you can. What you need me to do?" Miss Blue Eyes hugged me.

The next day she began telling me what it was like for her when she first came to Virginia: "I had no idea my husband's family were slave-holders. At first, he tried to explain it away, saying it was simply a way of life, but I couldn't believe the way colored people were being treated. The beatings, the squalor, the smells, the living conditions; it was all so repugnant. "My heart especially went out to the helpless little colored children; they were treated worse than animals. I saw the way they made mothers go back in the fields soon after giving birth. I watched as one of them cried out in agony after being forced to leave her baby in a pig troth and go work in the fields for hours; when she returned, her baby was covered with snakes.

It's simply inhumane! You can't treat people this way. It has to stop! Even though my husband grew up with slavery, he has since come to realize that it's wrong. He's a good man and knows it's time for slavery to be abolished. Negroes are people too and should not be exploited for their free labor."

Every time Miss Blue Eyes talk 'bout us she never call us *niggers*. Not once I ever hear her or Massa say the nigger word. Dat's all most white folks call us; hear it so much we call each udder nigger. Nigger a hateful word, and every time we say it, we shame ourselves and our own people who come long befo' us and died trying to be free. I swore to never say that awful word again and teach Precious to never say it.

Miss Blue Eyes said she was concerned about the number of slaves they've been moving in and out. "We need to get out as many as we can, as fast as we can". I thank God we've been able to keep our secret operation going for as long as we have but we need to be even more vigilant in order to maintain our secrecy." "How can I help, Miss Blue Eyes? I do whatever you tell me." I knew we could depend on you Mattie."First, we need to determine which Negroes want to be free from those who don't."Huh? I wanna make sho' I hear her right, so I asked "What you mean by Negroes who wanna be free"? Don't all Negroes wanna be free?"

"You'd be surprised. Many Negroes don't know or understand what freedom even means and will continue to believe that their present state is and always will be that of a slave. In order to free them from their physical chains, we must first free them from the mental chains that enslave their minds.

We need to separate slaves who can be trusted to take part in this life-saving endeavor from those who might put us at risk. Please understand; freedom isn't free and it could cost us our lives, so we need to make sure we don't get revealed by the very people we're trying to save." Miss Blue right, I know dat not all slaves can be trusted; not even with they own lives, cuz they minds' belong to whites, and they don't even know it. They content with their lowly slave status, and dat could be very dangerous for those trying to help 'em.

I went up to meet with Dori and Gray to see how I could lend a hand, but soon as they seen me coming, they began mocking me, using high voices; "Massa dey stealing yo slaves" as dey laughed. Said Massa told 'em erything I said 'bout 'em stealing his slaves. I hung my head in shame; I felt like such a fool. Then I hear 'em laughing, and when I looked up, I saw even Gray, the quiet twin, was cracking a rare smile. I asked them to forgive me; they said ain't nothing to forgive. "Shows you can be trusted, dat made me feel better. Dori said, "Don't know how much longer we can get away with this. Time ain't gonna be on our side fo' much longer. We need to be even more careful to make sure no one says something or does something that will bring attention to us."

The brothers told me they was more abolitionists not only round here but all through the South, both colored and white doing the same thing we doing. They call 'em conductors; they developed a network of secret routes that lead to freedom called the *Underground Railroad*. They ain't say who they was; say it best I don't know and they probably right. I know for sho' Miss Lillie ain't one. I been away from that evil woman almost a year now and hardly ever think 'bout her 'cept when Miss Blue Eyes told me she been asking for me, saying she want me and Precious back. I rather die than go back to Miss Lillie, so I quickly pushed that thought rat out my mind.

The brothers said since the start of the war most the young, healthy men round here joined the Confederate Army to fight the approaching Union armies. With less suspicious eyes around, they been able to keep their secret operation going, but dat don't mean we don't need to be careful. Many of 'em left their genteel wives to maintain the plantations, but most of those well-kept, sheltered white women don't know the first thing 'bout running no plantation, much less caring for slaves. The long-lasting war has become very costly for the South, and the Confederates have asked Southerners to provide money, food, and other things to support the war efforts. They encourage the women to sell off personal belongings, including their slaves, and many are willing to do so because it costs them too much to feed and house 'em. Massa Wilson is known for buying slaves, so there's always plenty supply. With so much attention being paid to the war, most white folks don't be thinking 'bout what's going on at the Wilson Plantation; that is, up until now. Massa told us 'bout a conversation he had with a few older town folks who was asking him 'bout the number of slaves we been selling off; he said he was able to settle their concerns but warned us to be even more careful. A new batch of slaves is coming up from Georgia, and they in a bad way; many of 'em been sold over and over. Some slaves who been sold over and over agin stop caring what may happen to 'em; special women who lost chillun and most they family, they just give up on life, dat's so sad. While others become so mean and angry, they hard to control. The mean ones really give colored slave drivers a hard time; believing they working for the white man against they own people. In most cases, dat's true, but they have no idea how different these boys is and will never know how close they came to being free, and that's a crying shame!

We ain't got time to deal with slave's who might give us trouble and bring attention to what we doing. We hurry and separate slaves by how they act and how fast they able to move; we don't have time to spare. Rowdy or crippled slaves get sent to auction right away. I feel bad, but the brothers quickly remind me; "*This is slavery, not a cakewalk.*" Miss Blue Eyes leaves it up to the brothers and me to choose who go and who stay, and we keep the slaves moving in and out as fast as we can. We don't give 'em time to think 'bout what's gonna happen to 'em. Before they know it, they either headed for freedom or back into slavery. It's troubling, but we ain't got no choice. Whenever I send a slave off to freedom, it makes me feel like I'm freeing myself. I know my time is coming soon, but for now, I use the amazing power I been given to free others. I just wish I could free 'em all, but many don't even know they slaves.

Misery Returns

Everything running smoothly; we keep moving slaves in and out. No sooner do we get new ones than we send off the old ones. Then one day while I was sweeping the parlor, out of nowhere, I got the strangest feeling, like somebody was looking at me. I slowly turned around and see Miss Lillie standing there, big as day and dark as night. I was so struck by the mere sight of her dat I jumped back; I couldn't believe my eyes. We both just stood there staring at each other for what seemed like a long time. She was glaring at me with the same hate and scorn she always did. She looked even worse than I remembered. I could tell she been drinking, her eyes red and she reeking of the smell of whiskey. I hurried and got myself together and said; "I'll go get Missus for you." Miss Blue Eyes came in the room "I'm right here, Mattie." I found out later that Miss Lillie showed up with no warning.

They said she just carried on, screaming 'bout how Miss Blue Eyes stole her slaves and she want 'em back or she was going to the law. She put up a big fuss. Miss Blue Eyes tried to reason with her, but she wouldn't let her get a word in edgewise. I just stood there, looking back and forth at both of 'em, trying to figger out what to do. The only thing I could think of was getting to Precious as quick as I could. I know if she see Miss Lillie, she will know something is terribly wrong, so I need to get to her. While they was still fussing, I ran out the parlor, calling for Precious. There was no sight or sound of her nowhere, but I keep on calling "Precious, where are you?" Then I see Miss Lillie's old beat-up carriage sitting in front of the house; a coachman was standing nearby and he had a strange look on his face. I passed him by, but then turned back and asked him "Where's my daughter? Where's Precious?" But he ain't say nuttin. Then I hear a sound a slight muffle, and it was coming from the barn. I quickly ran and threw the barn doors open. Inside was the wagon we use to haul slaves, and Gray was sitting up in it. Before I could ask, he said to me "Mattie, Precious is awright and you gonna be awright too." "What you mean, I gonna be awright too?" "Miss Lillie come for you and Precious". Miss Blue Eyes came running up and she was breathing hard. "Mattie, I'm so sorry, but we have to let you go Miss Lillie is causing a big stir, but don't worry. I promise I'm going to get you and Precious back as soon as I can." What? This can't be happening? I ain't wanna hear no more and went back to calling for Precious. "Where are you, Precious?" I heard Gray said "She right here, Mattie." I looked over and saw Precious peering through covers in the back of the wagon; I jumped in and pulled the covers back. A rag was over her mouth and ropes was tied round her hands and feet as she struggled to free herself. I pulled the rag away from her mouth and started loosening the ropes. "Gray, why she tied up, I asked"? Come, let her loose." But he ain't move. Miss Blue Eyes turned and ran out the barn holding her face in her hands and crying. Outta nowhere Miss Lillie's coachman come up from behind me, pushed me down, and commenced to tying me up. I was kicking and screaming; I squirmed to get close to Precious. "No, please don't let her take us back!" We screamed! "Somebody help us, please!" The wagon pulled off with us begging for mercy. Why is this happening? Ain't we been through enuff? I looked up at the bleak, dark skies and cursed toward the heavens "Damn you, God! Why don't you put an end this? How much longer we have to bear such pain? Every night, I fall on my knees and pray to you. Lawd, why you keep betraying us? Why, why you make us suffer so?" I was laying as close to Precious as I could, trying to keep us both calm, but we was too overwrought with grief.

The next day, was cold and pouring rain; it was as if the skies was crying for us. I welcomed the rain, cuz it washed away the dry tear stains dat was streaming down our faces. We cried all night; don't think we got no more tears left. We was holding on to each other for dear life and rocking back and forth. Eventually we got up; me and Precious started walking toward the God-forsaken house I hoped we'd never have to enter again. There, we found Miss Lillie; she was sitting by the fireplace. She ain't even turn to look our way when we came in. She said scornfully, "Go get me some firewood." We both turned round, but she stopped us. "No, let the girl go for it. You go fetch my shawl." I looked at Precious; I ain't wanna leave her alone. Before I left her side, I pointed her to a stack of firewood sitting out in the yard and coaxed her forward. She slowly let go of my hand and started walking toward the muddy yard. As I watched her walk away, I was thankful she had shoes on; they reminded me of a better life. I was still looking after her when Miss Lillie screamed at me "I said, go fetch my shawl!"

I ran off to look for it, but I ain't see it nowhere. I went upstairs and looked in all the rooms, but I still ain't see it. I think, Precious should be back with firewood by now, so I gave up looking for her shawl and ran back downstairs. When I got back to the kitchen, I saw Precious loading firewood in the hearth. She still had on the same dress they bring her back in; the sleeve was torn and ragged edges was hanging down. I shouted "Watch yo' sleeve, Precious!" and started moving toward her, but Miss Lillie stepped in front of me."Leave her alone. Time she learned how to fend for herself," and began tugging at my clothes.

As I tempted to pulled away, I yelled again "Be careful." Precious turned to look at me; that's when the fire caught hold of her sleeve. She jumped up screaming and running round the kitchen with her arm on fire. I went to go after her, but Miss Lillie was still trying to hold me back. I pushed her off me and she fell up against the wall. She yelled at Precious "Stop your screaming child!" I shouted "Stop, Precious, stop!"

and watched as she fell to the floor. I quickly ran to her, grabbed up a cloth sitting in a nearby chair and started hitting her arm to smother out the flames. After they went out, I wrapped the cloth round her arm and held it there til' it cooled down. I was still holding it when I looked at the cloth closer and saw it was the shawl Miss Lillie had sent me for. She had been sitting on it all along. I looked at my Precious as she cried softly looking at her arm as it was smoking. "Ma po' baby, ma po' baby" I cried. Miss Lillie pulled herself up and in the most cruel way said "Now you both got matching burns. Guess it's true what they say "The apple don't fall far from the tree after all." I jest looked at her; what a mean, ungodly woman! She's the devil outta hell! It took some time for Precious's arm to get better, and the skin was still red where the fire licked around it. Every day, I rub a piece of aloe plant on her scar to help it heal. One day as I was rubbing her arm, she looked up at me and said "Mammy, I'se glad I got a burn mark too, cuz it makes me look more like you." I kissed my sweet child; as I hugged her, I knew I need to get us away from here.

The other white ladies don't take up with Miss Lillie no mo'; they could tell she was poor white trash and a drunk on top of dat. Her overseers left after she stopped paying 'em and stole most of her livestock and other things. Several of her slaves ran away too, mostly young males. Most of the females have small children, and it's too hard to be on the run with children, so they forced to stay put. I can understand their plight, but I ain't gonna let that stop me. I know if I stay here much longer, I may kill or be killed, but if I make it to freedom, then it be worth it. Since we been back, Miss Lillie keeps a close eye on us. She moved us in the Big House and had her blacksmith put runaway shackles round our ankles so she can always hear where we at. They don't hamper our movement much, but they pinch and scar our ankles badly. Miss Lillie be drunk most the time, and when she fall off to sleep, we come and go as we please. These days, she drinks more than she eat and it's just as well, cuz ain't much food, least nothing worth eating. There's a little meal, bits of stale corn pone and some rotten-looking meat with fuzz growing on it. I think it used to be ham, but I won't eat it or let my Precious eat it. But I sho' would give it to Miss Lillie and hope it poison her; I hate that woman!

The field hands got a small vegetable patch down by slave row. The women forage for plants and the men hunt small animals, anything they can do to make do. Miss Lillie had dozed off in another one of her drunken stupors, so me and Precious went down to slave row. Me and the women, picked some greens, carrots and taters; we cooked up a good meal and fed the children; they all look so poorly. We share the same strife; being together gives us some comfort and makes us feel a little better. Even though we slaves and don't have much to smile 'bout, we still find ways to have a bit of fun. We laugh at how white folks dance with no rhyme or reason, like they having a conniption or sumptin'. Two men start kicking up they legs and acking the fool. I laughed so hard my side ached, *ewwwee.*

But most times, we talk about being free. There ain't a day goes by we don't think about freedom. *Slavery ain't something you ever get used to; it get used to you.*

The Demise

News travels fast from plantation to plantation. They told me how Miss Lillie caused a whole lot of ruckus telling anyone who listened dat Miss Blue Eyes stole me and Precious from her. Dat's what made the sheriff start sniffing round and asking the slaves questions. It ain't take 'em long to figger out what was going on, and brought everything to bear to shut it all down. They threw both Massa Wilson and Miss Blue Eyes in jail and threatened to kill Massa but didn't cuz he was one of dem, or so they thought and spared his life. After a brief court trial, they was both found guilty. They stole their money out the bank, took their land, furniture, livestock, and whatever else they wanted. They got rid of the slaves who was left; the old ones been with the Wilson's all they lives was given to udder plantation owners in the area, and the young, healthy ones was sold off. Worst of all, they took away Massa Wilson's right to be a lawyer and a senator, both things he loved to do the most. None of this went down without a powerful fight though. They said the twins Dori and Gray, fought fiercely along with other brave slaves and they had a shoot-out like no other. Said they dug trenches in the road, so when the sheriff and his posies came riding up, they horses fell over in the holes. Any white man who got close to the house, they shot and killed as many of 'em as they could before they overtook 'em. Sadly, Gray was lynched, but not before they cut off his fingers, toes, and his privates and sold pieces as keepsakes to the large gathering of white men who came to watch it all. Dori got beat so bad dat he lost a eye, then sold him further into slavery someplace called *New Ohleens,* I believe. I cried my eyes out listening to what happened to the Wilsons and the twin brothers. None of 'em warranted such a terrible demise; they tried to right a terrible wrong and died or nearly died trying. The Wilson's lost their entire fortune. Nobody seemed to know what come of Massa Wilson or Miss Blue Eyes; some said they moved back north to Philadelphia. They said they had to hold Massa back, as the brothers was beat and killed and helplessly watched as the house and land dat been in his family for generations went up in flames. Afterward, he collapsed in a heap; they said he went soft in the head and couldn't speak no more. What a shame! What a crying shame!

They found udder white folks in the area who was hiding slaves too, and they met the same terrible fate. I remember the brothers telling me 'bout other white abolitionists, but they never told me who they was and I'm glad they didn't, cuz it would just add to my sorrow even more. It seems like the few good white folks who tried to end slavery don't amount to the many bad ones who wanna keep it going. I don't know how they can call themselves Christians, go to church every Sunday, and pray for God's goodwill. When I think 'bout it, whatever they have is cuz we picked it for 'em, built it for 'em, cooked it for 'em, and took care of it for 'em, and all we got in return was more pain and suffering. Massa Wilson and Miss Blue Eyes don't care 'bout money and things; they care 'bout people, human beings black as we might be, but human nonetheless. They was good, caring, loving white folks and taught me no matter how bad things get, God will take care of me and all us slaves; God Bless 'em. Just like Miss Blue Eyes always said; "We're all God's children; white and black alike". No matter what happened to 'em; I know they never lost their kindness and mercy. I'm stronger in my faith and truly believe dat God will see us through this hell here on earth. Slavery is a sinful act and it must end, don't know when and don't know how but I do know nuttin' don't last always. One day, we will be free.

Miss Lillie sent me to town for some much- needed provisions. She stays too drunk to do dat herself anymo'. I taught Precious how to deal with her when I ain't round. I told her if she gets riled up to hide her bottle; pretty soon, she be begging you to help her find it and forget what she was mad about. At times, she be so drunk she can hardly stand up.

She shakily wrote out a note for me to give to the slave boy; he really a old man but whites still call him "boy"; he works for the white grocer. When I got to the grocery store, I give him the note and stood outside to wait for him to bring back the groceries. While I was standing there, some white ladies was cackling nearby. One of 'em said something 'bout the Wilsons, so my ears perked up but I kept my head down so as not to let on I was listening. Anudder one said "I hear Mrs. Wilson wants to leave Virginia and go back to Philadelphia, but she can't because her husband's too sick to travel."

What? Did I hear right? Could Massa and Missus still be round here? I was like a cat on a hot tin roof now, but I stayed calm and keep listening. "I heard they were staying out at the old Perkins place just outside of town by the creek while her husband recuperates." "Well, that's what they get for being nigger lovers." One piped up "I never liked her no way she was snooty and thought she was better than us I say good riddance!" "I place all the blame at her feet. She filled her husband's head with all her crazy Northern notions. His father, Judge Wilson, God rest his soul, raised him better than that. "He must be rolling over in his grave."

Listening to what they was saying, made me boiling mad; can't none of them hateful white women hold a candle to Miss Blue Eyes, or Massa Wilson for that matter. They blinded by hate and fear dat Negroes will be set free, but in due time, we will be whether they want it or not. The slave boy, man came back with the parcels of groceries. I said to him jest what Miss Lillie told me to say "Miss Lillie said put it on her tab." I quickly run off before he could come back with a reply or the white grocer come out. I know she probably still owe him from the last time. I hurried back to the house and prepared dinner. I took up a plate to Miss Lillie, but she was already sleep, so I just covered it over and left it by her bedside. I rushed down to slave row; I don't know where the old Perkins place is, but I'm gonna find out. I start asking round if anybody know where the Perkins place was. Soon, a old man said he knew 'xactly where it was, cuz he used to be a slave on they place a long time ago before he was sold to Miss Lillie's family. He spoke fondly of the old couple, saying Massa Perkins was a preacher and use to have services for the slaves all the time and Missus Perkins would secretly teach the slave children how to read and write. He said they place was 'bout ten miles away, next to the creek, just on the other side of the bend in the road.

Right then, I start planning our escape. Getting away from Miss Lillie is always on my mind. I plan to steal away at night while she sleeping. I don't think she gonna come after us no mo'; she ain't go after none her udder slaves. But first, we need to get these shackles off our ankles, cuz they make noise every time we move. White pattyrollers roam the roads round here at night with dogs, looking for runaway slaves and they be sho' to hear us. If they catch us with no papers or tags from our owner saying we 'llowed to be off the plantation, they let the dogs on us, whip us, then sell us off to anudder owner after they have they way with us, most likely. A female slave with a young child looks strange anyway, so we need to be even more careful. I'se skeered to death just thinking 'bout what could happen if we get caught, but freedom keeps pulling me forward. This is our only chance and we gotta take it. I just need to figger out how to get these shackles off. I can't go back to the slave Miss Lillie had put the shackles on us cuz he might tell. If there's one thing I learned over the years, you gotta be careful who you trust. If you tell a slave sumptin', even if they family, they will likely tell white folks. To get to the truth, whites will threaten to whip slaves; somebody bound to talk. Once a slave feel the lick of the whip crack cross they back enough times, they tell erything they know; even make up sumptin' if they think it stop the whippings. The shackles don't look that strong; they old and been used so much over the years they worn down in many places. A good swipe with sumptin' sharp, most likely crack 'em right open.

One day, when no one was round, I went down to the barn to look for sumptin' to break the shackles. I looked around, but I ain't see nuttin' that looked strong enough; then I spotted a tool hanging on the wall next to the horse shed. It was a small sickle-looking tool; I think it was used to shod horses. I took it down and started prying the shackle open; the mo' I pried, the mo' it opened up. But I ain't open it all the way, just enough so when I'se ready, I can pry it all off, and I do the same with Precious's shackle when the time comes. Somehow, I know if I can get to Miss Blue Eyes, she will help me get away from here for good.

Runaways

I pried the shackles off and we left in the middle of the night. We started out running so we could get as far away as fast as we can. After running a distance, we slowed up and started walking, and kept walking. The moon was high in the sky and provided just enough light to make out where we going. We kept deep in the thicket, trying not to make much noise. I skeered of snakes, but I don't let Precious know, cuz then she be skeered too, but I sho' hope we don't run into none. After a while, we stopped to rest a bit near the creek. I packed a bundle of dried food; taters, berries, nuts, and roots for us to eat along the way; we ate some vittles and drank some water. I looked over at my sweet Precious, who was sleeping like she ain't got a care in the world. I smiled and rubbed her head; she a wonderful child; been through so much in her young life, but she know her mammy gonna always take care of her. I 'cided that no matter what, if we get caught, they won't take us alive; I'll make sure of dat. This life ain't worth living no more if we have to stay with Miss Lillie. All a sudden, I hear a crackling sound in the woods, sumptin was moving round. What is it, man, snake, critter? Then I remembered that I stuck the sharp tool I used to pry open the shackles in my pocket, just in case I needed it. I took it out so I can be ready for whatever comes up on us. My heart was beating fast; I shook Precious woke in case we need to run. We sat still as rocks; couldn't hear nuttin' but our breathing, and fast beating hearts. Soon a family of rabbits came scampering by; a mother with her four little, fuzzy babies. I said to Precious, "See, they running away too, just like we is." She giggled and we hugged. "We gonna be awright, baby I promise, we be awright."

We keep walking hand in hand along the creek bank, cuz it runs right pass the Perkins place. We walked for a long time, seemed long enuff to cover ten miles. The sun was starting to come up; I couldn't believe we walked through the night. I don't think we got much longer to go, but we too tired to go any further, so we stopped for some rest. We was deep in the woods I found a patch of soft bushes for us to lie in; we curled up close together and fell off to sleep. When I woke up hours later, I laid there taking in our surroundings. The sun was high in the sky; we musta slept through most of the day. We drank some water, ate a little more, and set off again. Precious keeps asking me how much longer we gotta go, but I don't really know. I think we lost, but I don't let on; I don't need her to worry, cuz then she start to worry me. We shoulda been there by now. Maybe following the creek bank took us out of the way. I'm not sure which way to go now, so we jest keep heading in the same direction. Our food done run out and we starting to get hungry, but we drink some water and keep on walking. Up ahead, I see a bend in the road coming up. I remember the old man telling me the Perkins place was just beyond a bend in the road. We picked up our steps, careful to stay off the road. Thank God we ain't run into no pattyrollers. Gettin' dark again, but we keep walking. I ain't sho' if we heading in the right direction or not, but we can't stop; we've come too far to turn back. I see a gleam of light up ahead; I couldn't tell if it was a star or a house? As I got closer, I could make out a small farmhouse and smoke was coming out the chimney, so somebody must be in there. A lit lantern was in the front yard; I remembered how Miss Blue Eyes always had me leave a lit lantern out front at night too. Could this be the old Perkins place? Could this be where Miss Blue Eyes is? I found a safe spot for Precious, covered her up with some bush, and told her to stay put till I come back for her.

She start to cry; I told her to hush up; I hated to be so harsh with her; she been so brave. I took her little face in my hand and told her "Precious, I need you to be still a little longer, baby I'll be right back, I promise." I creeped slowly up to the house, to get a better look. When I got close, a dog started barking; I stopped dead in my tracks. The last thing I need is a dog ripping me apart after I done come so far. I put my hand on the tool in my pocket and prepared myself to do whatever I needed to do. As it turned out, the dog was no real threat at all; he stayed up on the porch and just kept barking. I think he was as skeered of me as I was of him. The door creaked open, but I still couldn't see nobody. Then what looked to be an old woman stepped out; she had a ragged shawl over her head that was covering her mouth and nose.

For some reason, I wasn't skeered no mo' and moved closer. When I got to the edge of the porch, I was able to see her eyes; they was the same blue eyes that made my heart leap so many years ago. The woman lowered her shawl and stretched out her arms to me. I ran to Miss Blue Eyes and we held on to each other for the longest time, crying and hugging. I felt our strength coming together, strength that will help us, and free us both.

The Reunion

I could see Miss Blue Eyes had been through sumptin and it took a real toll on her. She still had her good looks and of course those beautiful blue eyes, but whatever happened had clearly aged her. I went back for Precious and we went inside together. This small house won't even half the size of the house on the Wilson Plantation, but dat's all gone now. I spotted Massa Wilson sitting over in the corner. He looked much older; his hair was grey. He had a stubble beard, and he was stopped over like an old man. I walked over and laid my hand on top of his. "Massa Wilson, it's me Mattie. You 'member me, don't you?" But he just looked straight ahead, he didn't even blink. Miss Blue Eyes told me he ain't spoke since the day they killed Gray and took Dori away. When it was all over, he fell to his knees screaming; "It was the most agonizing scream I ever heard in my life," she said. He then passed out, and when he came to days later, he just laid there. "I couldn't reach him anymore he hasn't uttered a word since then. His mind was clearly gone. We always feared of being caught, thought about it all the time, but we couldn't stop. We had to do something to help those people." She told me how they would often lie in bed all night talking about what would happen if they got caught. "We didn't care so much about what would happen to us. We cared mostly about what would happen to the slaves. What if they took them all away? What would we do then? Before we knew it, we had talked through the night. As the sun rose, we looked out at the beautiful acres of land and saw large numbers of dutiful Negroes headed out to the fields to tend to their duties. We knew what we had was due to the Negroes, who made it all possible. There was no denying that. My husband and I both agreed slavery must end and we were going to do all we could to see to it that it did, no matter what. That's why we did what we did, and we would do it again. They can take away our land, our money, and kill our trusted friends, but they will never be able to change our beliefs. We hold to our beliefs that slavery is wrong and must end. It's just a matter of time." She went on to tell me 'bout the old couple Massa and Missus Perkins, who died a while back. "They were good friends of ours, like grandparents; they were abolitionists too. In fact, it was the Perkins who convinced us to become abolitionists. The Perkins hid many slaves until they could be slipped out and moved further north toward freedom. Those kind-hearted, old souls died within days of one another. After the sheriff found out they were working with us, they came after them. As soon as Rev. Perkins saw them coming, he dropped dead away. His heart simply gave out on him. Mrs. Perkins posed no threat, so they let her remain in the house. In a matter of days, she went to sleep and never woke up. They were married forty-five years. Their place was empty, so we moved in shortly after they burned our place down. I believe the Perkins would have wanted us to.

I began caring for Massa Wilson. Every day, I take him for walks so he could get his strength back. There was a chapel a few feet from the house, so I take him there and pray for him. I ask God to keep us safe and sound and return Massa to his right mind." Me and Precious go to the chapel to pray as well; it always comforts us. One day, Miss Blue Eyes came in and said she needed to speak with me, so I sent Precious outside to play with the dog. Her and the dog is best friends now; she even gave him a name "Dog," and he follows her everywhere she go. Miss Blue Eyes told me the Perkins had been teaching and praying with Negroes for years and truly believed we should be free as well as go to heaven. They were devoted to freeing slaves. The old man was a preacher of sorts, even though the only people who attended his church were the slaves.

Unbeknownst to most people, when Rev. Perkins built the chapel, he put tunnels underneath to hide slaves. He cut holes in the floor in the shape of small crosses so they could get air and covered them over with rugs. The tunnels served as a hiding place for hundreds of slaves who came through their property including the many we sent their way. "Only Master Wilson and I know about them, and now you know, but you must never tell anyone else not even Precious, unless it becomes absolutely necessary."

"They Comin' for You"

More than a month passed with no sight or sound of anyone coming after us; I begin to feel a little more at ease. Then one night, while I was settling Massa Wilson down for bed, I heard something rustling outside, and the dog started barking. Miss Blue Eyes was sound asleep; I ain't wanna to wake her up, cuz she don't often rest well no more. I grabbed the gun we kept in the corner opened the door, and stepped out on the porch. I shouted "Who there?" but I ain't hear nuttin'. "You better answer me, or I'm gonna start shooting and I'm bound to hit you."

Then I heard a slight voice say, "It me, Miss Mattie; Sammy."

"Sammy who?"

"Sammy from Miss Lillie's place."

"Miss Lillie? Come show yo'self." A young boy stepped out the shadows and started coming toward me, but I kept my gun trained on him. "Tell me why you here?"

He began telling me that his grandpa had sent him to warn me dat Miss Lillie was sending the sheriff to come for me and Precious.

"What?" I can't believe this woman still after us. "For God's sake" why don't this wicked woman leave us alone?" I brought the boy in the house and gave him sumptin' to eat and drink.

He kept talking "Miss Lillie always drinking, she keep ranting and raving 'bout getting you back. When you first left, she sent some slaves to look for you, they ain't really look dat hard. But when they came back and told her you was gone for good, she just wouldn't 'cept it. She kept pestering the sheriff to go after you, even after he told her you been gone too long and they don't know where to start to look. But she keep after em' anyway. She made him question all the slaves 'bout your whereabouts. When they got to my grandpa, he got skeered. They threatened to beat him first, but then they told him they was gonna beat my mama if he don't tell 'em where you at. He couldn't see his daughter get beat she just had a baby, so he tells all he know. Later, he had me sneak away to come warn you. You betta leave here fast, Miss Mattie, cuz they comin for you." This is troubling news. But there was always something I wondered 'bout, so I asked the boy "How long it take you to get here?"

"Not long," he said. "First, I swim cross the creek, then I run through the brush so no one could see me. It ain't take me no time at all." *Hmmm*, I thought to myself or a minute befo' rushing off to tell Miss Blue Eyes what the boy had said. She began wringing her hands and pacing back and forth. "I'm so afraid they will burn this place down just like they did ours. What are we going to do? My husband can't survive another skirmish. This could kill him, if they don't kill us first." The next morning, we was still talking 'bout what to do when in the distance, we heard what sounded like horses headed our way. Miss Blue Eyes told us to go to the chapel. I knew what she meant and quickly grabbed up our things. Me and the children ran to the chapel and went down in the tunnels. I couldn't hear too well down there, but I could feel the horses getting closer. The horses stopped; they must be at the house now. I heard someone shout for Miss Blue Eyes.

"Mrs. Wilson, please come out or we will have to come in after you."

I hear Miss Blue Eyes say, "What do you want sheriff?"

The sheriff said; "We come for the slaves you hiding here."

"What slaves?"

"You know, the ones that run away from Miss Lillie's place."

"I have no idea what you're talking about," she said.

"Don't you lie to me,". "You and your husband have been hiding slaves long enough and it's time you stopped!" Miss Blue Eyes shouted back "My husband is ill. We no longer have any means to hide slaves You took care of that. Need I remind you? Please go and leave us alone. You've done enough." The sheriff ordered some of his men to go inside and search the house.

I ain't hear nuttin' for a while, then somebody said; "Ain't no sign of 'em in there, Sheriff just Mr. Wilson sitting in the corner drooling; looking like a shadow of his former self." Then the dog started barking; he was right above us; he musta followed us into the chapel after I told Precious she couldn't bring him with us. His barking got their attention, cuz I hear footsteps in the chapel. The dog started growling as they got closer to our hiding place. One of 'em said; "If he comes after us, shoot him!" I felt Precious jump, so I put my hand over her mouth to keep her quiet. The closer they moved toward us the more the dog growled. Dog is friendly most times; he never goes after nobody. It's lak he could tell these men was there to cause us harm and he was trying to protect us. His barking and growling got louder, then we heard a gunshot; we all jumped, but we ain't make a sound, cuz it could cost us our lives. Dog yelped, then it went quiet; they shot him. I felt Precious' tears roll over my hand as I held it over her mouth. They kept moving closer to the tunnel entrance, but it was hidden; if you ain't know it was there, you wouldn't know, cuz it looked like part of the floor boards. They kept walking across our heads; back and forth, back and forth. Then outta nowhere, they started kicking over the altar and the pews. What nasty bastards they don't even respect the Lord's house. The sheriff hollered "What ya'll doing in there? Come on out, you sacrilegious fools!" When they left the chapel, we all took a huge sigh of relief but still kept quiet. Miss Blue Eyes yelled at them for killing her dog and told them how rude and disrespectful they were of the deceased Rev. and Mrs. Perkins. "Disgraceful!" And demanded they leave the property immediately. The sheriff apologized for his men's actions, but before he left, he warned Miss Blue Eyes not to hide anymore slaves or she will suffer the same consequences or worse; then, they all rode off. We stayed down in the tunnel for a long time before Miss Blue Eyes came for us; she wanted to make sure they were gone. She had fixed some food and we all ate together; I feed Massa Wilson, his hands too shaky to feed hisself.

Several weeks passed; we spend much of our time talking 'bout how we was gonna get away from here. We feared the sheriff was coming back. We both were so tired of this madness. I asked her; "Why Miss Lillie so hell bent on getting us back?" "For the same reason most Southern whites want to keep slavery going. They see Negroes as property that they can use as they please, while continuing to gain wealth for themselves and their families for generations to come. What they are doing is wrong. They simply cannot continue to enslave people. It must stop!" While she was talking, I thought I heard horses coming again.

"Shhhh, Miss Blues Eyes, they coming back!" Me and the children hurried back to the chapel; as we was leaving, I saw Miss Blue Eyes reach for the gun. This could be it, I thought to myself. This may be the end of the line for all of us; we may die this time. I'll take death over going back to Miss Lillie; I ain't never going back to her; never and I mean it. It's a shame, but I gotta take the children with me; I can't leave 'em behind to suffer no mo'. Outta nowhere, I hear a thunderous sound of horses getting closer and closer; sounded like a cavalry coming!

Why in heavens name do they feel the need to send so many after a poor slave woman and a young girl? I hear Miss Blue Eyes scream. It was a terrible, loud scream. Dear God I nevah thought I would have to sit by and listen as Miss Blue Eyes was killed. How awful! Me and the children was sitting there shaking, waiting to be found out. I put my hands over they eyes and told 'em to keep 'em shut tight, and I did the same. I don't want my last sight to be of my killers; I just pray they hurry and put me out my misery. But befo' I let these bastards kill us, I will kill the children myself then take my own life. I seen enough of my babies die; only this time, it will be at my own hand. I'se so sorry but I gotta do it, *sniff*. While I was still thinking the most horrible thoughts I hear a man's voice call out my name, "Mattie!"

Who dat? I wondered. Have I died and ain't feel a thing?, But I can still feel myself and I still breathing, so I must still be alive!

I hear my name again. "Mattie!" Is dat God calling me home?

The tunnel door suddenly opened and a gush of fresh air came rushing in. I squeezed the children closer to me and took the tool out my pocket; I was just about to cut all our throats. I was prepared to leave this awful life, once and for all. Then I hear the man's voice again "Mattie, come on up here, girl!"

Who dat keep calling my name? Who could it be? I opened my eyes a little and looked up. The sun was shining in my eyes, so I could only make out a shadow; it appeared to be a colored man with a patch over his eye. Lawd, I done died and went to heaven, low and behold; God is a colored man!

Then the ghostly man said "You coming up or do I have to come down there for you?" The children quickly jumped out my arms before I could stop 'em, and scampered up the steps.

Now, I was left sitting there all alone not knowing if I was dead or alive. "Come on up here, girl." I was so skeered; I slowly start climbing up the steps. Before I even reached the top, the man pulled me straight up like I was a straw doll. When I got to my feet, I saw his smile; I know that smile. I screamed "Oh my God! Dori is that you?" He smiled even broader. "It is you. It's really you!" He hugged me tight and I hugged him tight right back. I could hardly believe my eyes. "How you get here? Thought you was sold away?" I keep asking him questions as he pulled me toward the house. When we got inside, I see Miss Blue Eyes standing amongst a large group of white men, and they was all hugging.

As soon as she saw me, she came running over. "Mattie, these are our friends. They came all the way from Philadelphia. The war is over and the North won. You're free. All the slaves are free! They've come to take us all away from here. We're safe, we're finally safe." Everyone let out a Yankee yell "YeeHaa", but I still don't quite understand what was going on, so I just sat back and listened as the men talked 'bout hearing what happened to their dear friends, the Wilsons and the twin brothers. They knew Dori and his twin brother Gray from when they lived in Philadelphia with Massa Wilson as free, educated men. When they found out that Dori was boarded on a boat in New York harbor bound for Louisiana they overtook it and freed him along with other slaves with him at the time. Then they took Dori to Philadelphia and nursed him back to health. Other than losing his eye in that terrible fight, he looked in fine shape. He remained there, hidden in plain sight, and now he's here to free us. God is good! They tell me they got plenty colored folks walking around Philadelphia who come and go as they please. Just the thought of that makes me feel so good.

I looked over and saw a load of slaves, seem lak I know 'em. Just then, the young slave boy yelled "Mammy! Grandpaw!" and ran over to the group. That's when I seen they was Miss Lillie's slaves; all sixteen of 'em. I ran over and started hugging 'em all.

"How y'all get here? How y'all get away from Miss Lillie?"

Dori said "We took 'em."

"What you mean, you took 'em? I thought; "Oh no, she gonna come after all us."

Then the boy's Grandpaw said "Miss Lillie ain't coming for nobody ever again not since Lucifer come for her."

They all started chanting *"Loose here, Devil, loose here, loose here, Devil, loose here."* Everyone was shouting and dancing around, even

Precious. I grabbed her hand and we danced together. While we was having a joyous time, I looked over and saw Massa Wilson standing in the doorway. Miss Blue Eyes ran to hold him up, but he was standing strong and tall on his own. He was trying to say sumptin; I quiet everybody down.

"*Shhh,* quiet! Massa trying to talk."

He called out for Dori and reached out his hand toward him. He said softly "Dori, where you been?"

Dori answered loudly "I been here all along, Boss Where you been?"

We all broke out in huge laughter. Massa smiled faintly; I think he finally come back. The next day, we was all packed up and headed north to freedom.

Thank you, Lawd; you ain't forsake me after all. I knew you wouldn't. I laid back in the wagon grinning from ear to ear, looking up as the clouds rolled by. As I looked up at the clear blue skies, I wondered if the clouds in Philadelphia look the same as they do in here in Virginia? I don't know, but I'm sho' 'bout to find out.

The End

CHAPTER 2
Beaufort, South Carolina, 1859

LUCY AND MISS SUSIE

My name is Lucy, and when I was growing up on the Fairwell Plantation, I had no idea I was a poor slave girl. That's because I was raised right along with my white mistress; Miss Susie and we was real close. My mammy been with Miss Susie's family since she was a young girl. She was a house slave and raised Miss Susie from the time she was born. We're both about the same age, born just months apart; I'm the youngest. Growing up, Mammy used to tell us stories about how she nursed us both, often at the same time. She said Miss Susie would take her tit right out my mouth and put it in hers. Miss Susie laughs out loud every time my mammy tells us that story; I laugh too. We be together all the time, and what Miss Susie do, I do too. When she said words, I said the same words. When she eat, I eat; when she cry, I cry too even if I don't know why we crying. When other children were around, we still played together, we like our own company best. I was closer to Miss Susie then I was to any slave children. Mammy said I ain't need to be round no nigger children anyhow. I live in the Big House along with my mammy, but I sleep in Miss Susie's room on the floor next to her bed sometimes underneath. When her clothes and shoes don't fit or she just don't want them no more, I gets her handme-downs, so I was always dressed better than other slave children. If she had a ribbon in her hair, she had Mammy put one in mine too. Some say we bear a 'semblance, 'cept she white and I colored, but my skin light, almost white.

Once Mammy heard me and Miss Susie say we was sisters. She scold us both and told us to stop saying it, but when she ain't in earshot, we say it anyhow. A old slave mammy once told me Miss Susie daddy was my daddy too, but he don't treat me like he do her; he mostly ignores me. When I told my mammy what she said, she got real mad. "That old woman needs to mind her own bizness". She grabbed me by my shoulders and told me to never speak about it again, and I never did. As we got older, my own mammy won't able to say nothing about my comings and goings, cuz Miss Susie was in charge of me, and where she go, I go too. The time came for Miss Susie to go to school, and when she came home, she would teach me everything she learned. We read books together every day, but we have to keep it secret, cuz colored children ain't 'llowed to learn to read or write, so no one know I could not even my own mammy. I loved Miss Susie and she loved me too, cuz we sisters, *Shhh!*

Years passed; Miss Susie don't seem to want me round much no more. She got new playmates now white girls, and they ain't take to me the same way she did when we was young. They ain't very nice to me; treat me mean and order me round like they do other slave girls, but I ain't like other slave girls; I belongs to Miss Susie. One day when Miss Susie left me alone in a room with them, her white friends held me down and poured talcum powder all over my face and head. When she came back, she saw them all laughing at me and saying "Your face may look white, but you still black and ugly," and kept on laughing. She looked sad for a just bit, but she ain't say nothing; then she began laughing with them. I felt so shame. I don't know what got into Miss Susie. Why is she acting this way toward me? When I told my mammy what happened, she said to stay away from Miss Susie and her friends.

"And don't go round them less she call for you."

When Miss Susie turned thirteen, she had a big birthday party. I stood aside and kept my place just like my mammy told me too. I watched her and her friends giggle as she tore open her many gifts. I couldn't help but think about a time when she would always share her things with me, but those days is long gone now. One of her gifts was a shiny, silver comb, brush, and mirror set that she kept on her dressing table; it was the prettiest thing I had ever seen. Something else came with it a short, thick, white leather strap with a matching, fancy silver handle. *What she s'posed to do with that?* I thought to myself. I never asked, but I would soon find out.

Miss Susie had long, lovely yellow hair. She likes me to brush it and I enjoy brushing it for her. My hair is long too but not nearly as long or straight as Miss Susie's and it sure ain't yellow. Sometime when no one's around, I wrap a white rag around my head and throw it back and forth, like Miss Susie do her hair. Every night before she goes to bed, she has me brush her long tresses. I still enjoy being around her, but I could tell she ain't care so much for my company no more unless she wants me to do something for her. One night, while I was brushing her hair, she seemed moody and got real angry with me, but I ain't know why. Out of nowhere, she started screaming at me for not putting things back like I found them. Before I could say anything, she picked up that fancy leather strap and struck me hard cross my face with it. I just stood there, rubbing my cheek and staring at her. I couldn't believe she did that to me. But when I looked in her face, I saw nothing but rage and hate. From that point on, I knew she won't the same person I grew up with; she had changed, I didn't know it at the time but I had to change too.

Miss Susie went off to boarding school in Atlanta. I stayed on at the Big House with my mammy, who kept teaching me how to take care of rich white folks. She told me to watch the refine white ladies that come around; learn how they speak, how they act, and to mimic their ways. My mammy told me as a fancy yellow gal, I would be even more valuable to my owners if I was more refined and be less apt to sell me off. I kept up my learning while Miss Susie was away at school, but always behind closed doors. She left plenty of books in her room, and whenever I get a chance, I go in there and read, making out like I was keeping her room tidy. I let my mammy know I could read and write; she was real happy, but warned me to be real careful. She said if white folks find out, they might fix it so I never read again, maybe put my eyes out. That scared me so bad I don't dare let on to nobody.

Two years passed before Miss Susie returned home, and when she did, she had grown into a beautiful, refined young woman. She wore lovely clothes, talked much better than she used to and had fancy ways about herself. I hoped she could see I had changed too; she might treat me better. It didn't seem to matter, because she soon made me understand that I was her slave, not her friend and certainly not her sister, probably never was. Miss Susie was a respectable, rich white woman now, and I was just a poor slave girl, no matter how fancy, how yellow, or how smart, and that's all I will ever be. Soon after returning home, she began courting Massa Charles Taylor a short, fat man with bad teeth. His family owns the nearby Taylor Plantation. I remember him as a boy and knew he always had a shining for Miss Susie. I was a bit surprised when they announced their engagement, given her good looks, because she could do so much better than him. They daddies was longtime friends and his family has money. That's how white folks do; their children marry each other so they can keep the wealth amongst themselves. Miss Susie and Massa Charles had a big wedding, and many rich white folks traveled miles to attend the nuptials. Somebody told me I was given to them as a wedding present. When I heard that, I got real scared, cuz I never been away from my mammy before and went running to tell her.

She said to me "Child, you know Miss Susie well as she knows you, you be just fine. They plantation just a stone's throw away from here and we get to see each other by and by when they visit one another." Massa Taylor's daddy gave him and his new wife, Miss Susie, the family farm and a few slaves. Miss Susie put me in charge of running the house, because she knows my mammy trained me well. I went about setting up the household, but I soon see they gonna need more slaves to help out round here and I tell her so. It wasn't long before Massa Taylor went off for a while, and when he returned, he had a wagonload of niggers; can't say how many they was, though. Inside the wagon was a bunch of crying women, screaming children, and some nigger men towed behind in chains. It was an awful sight! My heart went out to those poor black souls; they looked so scared and helpless, not knowing what's to come of them.

My eyes locked onto one of the male slaves. He was in real bad shape; he had raw brandings on his chest and a number of open and bleeding lashes crisscrossing his back. He had the most angry look on his face; like he might strike you if you got too close, but the heavy iron chains on him held him at bay. I felt so sorry for him and kept staring at him, but my stare was broken when Miss Susie called for me to go care for the female slaves and the children. I took them all down to the creek, gave them some lye soap, and told them to wash their bodies. They sure is a stinky bunch! I gave them all clean flour sacks to wear until we could find more proper clothing for them. I fixed them up some slop made of salt poke, 'lasses, oats, and potatoes. I rang the slave bell and they all came running. While they was eating out the pig troths, I saw the same young nigger man I had seen earlier. He was chained under the smokehouse; red ants was crawling all over his body and biting him bad. When no one was watching, I threw a bucket of water on him to wash away the ants and help soothe his aches and pains. He just glared at me, but I could tell it made him feel better; I think I even saw a slight nod of gratitude.

I sneaked the angry slave some decent food from the Big House and he ate like they was no tomorrow. As I watched him eat, I see sumptin very different in this man. He ain't no common slave, he's prideful, he don't 'cept being a slave. With extra slaves, the Taylor Plantation is up and running. The field hands up early tending the fields, and I keep the house slaves on task, cooking, cleaning, and taking care of all the house duties. Many of the females Massa bought was specting; that give him more slaves to add to his stable. Miss Susie keeps going round rubbing they bellies. They went into labor, one rat after the udder. I ain't know nothing about birthing no babies, so I stepped aside and let udder slave women handle dat, but I help out where I can. Every time one of 'em go into labor, Miss Susie rat there watching the births. Don't know why she so awestruck by 'specting women and babies.

Big George

Dat pitiful-looking slave I helped a while back don't look so pitiful no mo'. He gained much of his strength back, not that he ever lost any. They call him Big George; he's a big, black, sturdy buck and his large muscles show through his ragged shirt every time he moves. He must be a Afrikin Dingo; cuz he large and tall like 'em. He look to be 'bout my age; hard to tell though cuz he keep a scowl on his face most times, but when he do smile, he show off a mouff full of pearly white teeth. Massa made Big George a field hand, but he ain't pick no cotton; they have him carry the big bags of cotton the udder slaves picked, turn them into bales, then hoist 'em up on wagons, and he do all this by hisself.

When I take the field slaves supper, I stop and watch Big George go about his chores, toting and bailing, bailing and toting; he's like a machine, never seems to tire. You can see he's angry, but he keeps it inside; he ain't cause no trouble least not yet. One day, I overhear Massa Charles talking to the overseer 'bout Big George, told him he wants Big George trained to be a prize fighter to fight udder slaves so he can take wagers on him. Pretty soon, the overseer have George pulling the plow round the fields like a mule for hours on end, cutting down trees, and carrying huge logs up to the Big House, then chop 'em up for firewood. Again, he don't grow weary; he jest keep on going; he one strong nigger. When he come round the back of the house to drop off firewood, I offer him water and something to eat. I try to have a talk with him, but he jest nod as I do most the talking.

I tell him 'bout myself and my own sorry life so he don't feel I'm meddling. After while, he opened up some.

He told me when he was a boy, he was a African prince, before the slavers came, kidnapped him, and brought him cross the ocean. Said his real name was Eqquos, but the white man won't let him use his given name and beat him every time he say it. But he don't care no mo' what slave name they call him; most times, they call him nigger and he ain't dat either, so it don't matter. In his mind, he still Prince Eqquos, and no white man can ever take that away from him. I never met no nigger like him befo', and if truth be told, he ain't no nigger at all; he a proud Afrikin man. He run away every time they sell him; said he been sold so many times he can't count no mo'; but the brandings and lashes all over his body is proof enough. He told me he fought off dogs, niggers and even the white men when they came after him. The whippings may have slowed him down some but I can tell he's just biding his time til he get a chance to runaway again. I tell him "Big George, ain't nowhere to run and nowhere to hide." But he ain't pay me no never mind; he seem 'termined to go back to Africa. I shook my head and thought to myself; what a damn fool slave!

Massa Charles left on another one of his long treks. Now, the overseer in total charge and he's a real mean "*redneck cracker.* We call him that under our breath, cuz he quick to use the whip, and when he gets mad, his face and neck turns red. He gives all the slaves a hard time, cracking the whip on men women even children at times. Night after night he goes down to slave row; rape the women and girls in front of the men folks and dare 'em to say or do sumptin. He's one nasty bastard. Big George hates him and let's him know it too every chance he get. One time, he reared back like he was gonna crack George with the whip; George looked him dead in his eye, like he dare him. That cracker backed down and left him lone too.

As time went on, me and Big George started to have feelings for each other. Whenever we get a chance; we sneak away to spend time together. George makes me feel like no man ever did befo'. His mere touch makes my skin tingle all over, and when he kisses me, I feel like I might blow up. We start to set up times so when he comes round to the back of the house to chop wood, I make sure to be in the kitchen. Sometime when he don't know I'm looking I stand back and stare at him. I watch as his strong body drips with sweat as he keeps chopping wood; every time he chops, I feel a stirring between my legs, like I'm the wood and he's the axe. *Lawd ha mercy!* Pretty soon, we give into our feelings and take each other. He covered my body with tender kisses, from my mouff, to my neck, my breasts, all over my belly, then between my legs. I calls out for Jesus, but not cuz I need help. I just don't want him to stop; I can handle this man all by myself. I arch my body to take in as much of George as I can. *Umm ...* they don't call him Big George for nuttin'. I ain't never felt lak this befo'. I can't get enuff of this man, want him all the time, but we need to be careful, cuz if Miss Susie find out we been together, she might make us stay away from each other, or worse, she might sell him off, and I couldn't bear that. So when we round others, we sneak looks, smiles, and touches, careful not to let on we lak each other.

Send Him Up!

Big George was out back one day chopping wood, and Miss Susie came in the kitchen. She stood in the back doorway looking out. First, I thought she was looking at the lovely zinnias in the garden like she sometimes do but then I see she ain't looking at no flowers; she looking at George. The mo' she stared at him the mo' worked up she seem to git.

She started to shift from one foot to the other; her face and neck was moist as she rubbed her hands cross her mouth and chest. If I ain't know no better, I'd swear I heard her let out a slight moan as her fingers lingered over her privates. Most times, white women look at nigger men like they scared of 'em or hate 'em, then turn they nose up at least when they in public. If I ain't know no better, I think Miss Susie looking at George in a lustful way, *hmmm*.

The next day, Miss Susie had me go summon George to the house said she needs him to move some furniture in her room. Old Abraham, the house nigger; he carrys out dem kinda chores most times, so I wonder why she need George. Maybe she think Abraham too old; he is kinda 'crepit. Anyway, I run to go fetch George; I find him bathing in the creek. I stood there for awhile taking in his black nakedness. My God, what a fine man he is! When he turned around and saw me he beckoned for me to join him. I threw off my garments and ran into his open arms.

He caught me lak I was a butterfly landing on his big, burly chest; he wrapped my legs round his waist. He kissed me deeply and shoved his long, hard manliness inside me. Ummm! Our bodies became one and we faded away in utter pleasurement.

I don't know how long we went at it; I just know I ain't want it to end. We laid entwined in each other's arms. Then I remembered, I'm s'posed to be fetching George for Miss Susie! I ain't tell him 'bout Miss Susie looking at him; I 'cided to leave that for another time. We hurried up and got dressed. I ran up ahead, cuz I ain't want nobody to know we was together. He went round to the back door, and I went to let Miss Susie know he was there.

When I told her, she said to me "Send him up." Huh? Send him up where? To her bedroom? Dat's odd; George ain't no house nigga, for her to have him upstairs, much less her bedroom, just ain't proper, ain't proper at all. I go tell George what she said and pointed him toward the back servants' stairs, but I followed close behind him. When we reached her door, I knocked and told Miss Susie he was there. She said "Come in," and we both entered, but when she turned around and saw me, she quickly told me "No, not you, just George!"

What's going on? I asked maself. George slowly stepped inside; I hear Miss Susie tell him to close the door behind him. I stood outside for a while trying to hear what was going on inside, but I ain;t hear nuttin', so I went back downstairs, but my mind was never far from what was going on upstairs. I keep running to the stairwell and looking up at Miss Susie's bedroom door. I still ain't hear nuttin', no talking, no furniture moving, not nuttin. After a long time, the door opened. I stayed behind the wall so I can't be seen. Then I hear footsteps on the stairs; must be George, so I run around back. At first, he was walking real slow, but by the time he got to the middle of the stairs, he picked up his steps, and by the time he got to the bottom, he was moving so fast he jest 'bout knocked me over when I stepped out. He ran past me, he kept going and headed straight for the back door.

I tried to run after him, but he was moving too fast. He jest kept running clear cross the field until he disappeared in the woods. What happened? Why he running so? Then I hear Miss Susie call me; she told me to heat up some bath water and bring it up. When I took it up, I poured some in the tub, leaving a little in the basin, so she could wash her face like she always have me do, but this time she told me to pour it all in the tub, so I did. Miss Susie was standing behind the dressing screen when I came in, and when she stepped out, she was completely naked.

I seen Miss Susie's naked body plenty times befo', but her body looked different this time. It was red and flushed all over, lak she was stung by a hundred bees, and she had a look on her face as if she had a spell put on her. She walked over to the tub and slowly let her body sink into the warm, soapy water. I picked up the soap to wash her back, again like I always do, but she said "Not now. I just wanna sit here for a bit," and motioned for me to leave. As I slowly closed the door behind me, the furniture Miss Susie said she wanted George to move was still in the same place; ain't nuttin' move a inch.

I could hardly wait to talk to George, but it was almost dinnertime and I need to start cooking. After I served dinner and cleaned up, I ran down to slave row to look for George. I keep asking round "Ya'll know where Big George is?" but no one seemed to know. I looked 'round for some time, but I couldn't find him nowhere, so I just gave up and headed back to the Big House. The next day, I ain't see George at all. I ain't spot him in the fields out back, nowhere. We was running low on firewood; I see the overseer, so I asked him "Suh, you know where George is? Firewood gitting low."

He answered me gruffly "Then cut some yourself; George busy."

"Yessuh."

A few days passed and George come back; I was so happy to see him I ain't care where he been, just glad he back. I waved to him from the back door, but I don't think he saw me, so I called out to him "Hey, Big George, where you been? Firewood low."

He waved back, but he ain't come up; he sent another nigger with some firewood, then he went off again. Umm, dat's strange!

After dinner, Miss Susie had already retired to her room, so I went back down to slave row to see if I could find George again. I ain't care no more, what folks said 'bout us; they can think what they want; I just need to know George whereabouts. I ask everybody I see, but they all say they don't know where he is, so I head back. As I approach the Big House, I saw a flicker of light coming from Miss Susie's bedroom window. When I got closer, I could make out two figures behind the lace curtains. They was standing close together real close. Then they was gone. Who could be with Miss Susie in her bedroom this time of night? Massa Taylor the only man I know to be with her at this hour, and that ain't often cuz they don't sleep in the same bedroom. Miss Susie said she prefer they have separate bedrooms; he slips in and out every now and then but he still away, far as I know.

I creep up and sit still on the back steps. After a while, who I see come out fixing his britches but Big George. I can't believe my eyes! I jumped up; he surprised to see me. In a whisper, I asked him "What you doing comin' out Miss Susie room this time of night? Thought you already moved her furniture?"

He just looked at me wildly, then lowered his head and said "She had me do sumptin else."

"What else?" I asked. But he pushed me aside and left in a hurry. I ain't go after him this time; I just watched as he walked away fast. I went upstairs to see if Miss Susie needed me to turn her bed down. But when I looked in on her, she was already fast asleep. Her bed clothes was all mussed up; Miss Susie a sound sleeper, and as a rule, she don't muss up her bed like dat. I quietly moved 'bout the room picking up her clothes that was strewn all over. I picked up her corset and sumptin' caught my eye; it was a button and it looked familiar.

I picked it up to have a closer look. I stared at it. Then it came to me; the button was from Big George's overalls. *Mmmm.*

The next morning, I went back upstairs to see if Miss Susie wants me to bring a tray up to her or if I should set the table. Much to my surprise, she was already up, dressed, and in fine spirits too. She was smiling and very pleasant; she was almost singing her words.

"Good morning, Lucy. What's for breakfast?"

"Anything you want, Miss Susie."

"Just bring me some orange juice for now," she said as she put her long hair up on top her head.

I said, "Yes'm," and slowly backed out the door. I can't get over what I seen last night; it don't seem real. Did I dream it? I wonder. I took the button out my pocket and was looking at it; when I hear Miss Susie come in the kitchen, I hurried and put it away.

"Lucy, I'm going to town today and I need you to accompany me."

Later on, the buggy pulled up, to my surprise Big George was steering the horses top hat and all! He had on the coachman's clothes, but they don't fit him. He was just about busting out the jacket, and the pants way too tight, but he somehow squeezed his big ass in 'em. Miss Susie was dressed in a fancy frock I never seen befo' that showed off her ample bosom. When she stepped out on the porch, George jumped down and opened the carriage door for her. He held out his arm, Miss Susie grabbed hold of his big muscle arm and climbed in.

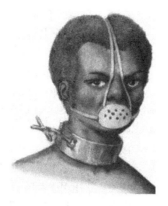

I climbed up top and took the seat next to George. He come up, snapped the reins, and the horse took off. We ain't look at each other or say a word; we both just stared straight ahead. The only sound was the horse's feet clomping along the sandy road. When we got to town, George hurried and climbed down to help Miss Susie out the carriage; I climbed down the best I could and stood aside to wait for Miss Susie's orders.

I always dread going to town, cuz Miss Susie always make me wear a collar round my neck that she attaches to a leash and leads me round why I carry her parcels. It makes me feel so shamed. Even though I'se a slave, I still human, not a dog, and don't wanna be treated lak one. No sooner had I thought, it she pulled the collar out her bag and handed it to me.

"Here, Lucy, put on this collar."

I took it and for a minute I looked at the delicate, brass collar with a heart-shaped key locket and fancy markings on it. I thought to myself, How could something so pretty be so ugly at the same time? No sooner had I locked the collar round my neck dat Miss Susie hooked on the leash, gave it some lead, and commenced to pulling me behind her. As I was being pulled, I took a quick glance at George, who was still standing there holding the carriage door open; he seemed to be beckoning for me to climb inside so he could carry me away from this humiliation. Miss Susie glided into the general store speaking to everyone as she passed, asking how they kinfolks was doing, and waving her hankie with her gloved hand. All the white gentlemen bowed and tipped their hats as she passed by. The white ladies greeted her, and they all passed small talk back and forth for a while as I stood aside with my head down. Then Miss Susie elegantly strode into the store.

"Afternoon, Mr. Sullivan. How I love the wonderful smells emanating from your fine groceries" she lilted.

"Thank you, ma'am."

"Mr. Sullivan, I'll have five cups of flour, four cups of sugar," then she stopped and looked back at me. "Lucy; how we fit for cinnamon? I want you to make one of your delicious peach pies."

"We could use some more, Miss Susie."

"Fine, give me a cup of cinnamon too." Then she spotted something. She squealed "Oooo, how pretty!" And with no warning at all, she snatched the leash, pulling my neck long with her; it hurt so bad. She began picking through a bunch of handkerchiefs and pulled out a few. Then she shouted to the grocer's slave "Boy, give me ten of these hankies Lucy, put them in your basket."

Oh, Lawd, I forgot and left the basket in the carriage. When she see I ain't have it, she gave me a nasty look and rolled her eyes. She called for George, and right away, he came running. "Go fetch Lucy's basket."

"Yes'm." He slyly looked over at me with sad eyes before running off.

Soon as we got back to the house, I started cooking and baking, because Massa Taylor was due home the next day, and Miss Susie said she wanted everything to be perfect for his arrival. Everybody was hustling and bustling; the house slaves was busy sweeping the floors, polishing the silver, and pounding out the rugs. The field hands was pulling and picking the crops, so when Massa Taylor turns into his plantation, he could see his bounty all ready for market. George brought up a load of firewood lak he always do. I went out to fetch some, but I ain't say nuttin' to him. I could feel his eyes on me, but I ain't give him as much as a peek. We ain't spoke, and I ain't fixing to start now, cuz I'm way too busy. Massa Taylor arrived the following day; all the slaves was lined up along the road smiling and waving jest like the overseer told 'em to do. He had with him four wagons full of supplies, farm equipment, and two big oxen following along.

I stood on the porch behind Miss Susie. When he reached the front of the house, she ran to the wagon. "What you bring me, Taylor? I can't wait to see what you bring me." Dat's so like her, not even as much as a hello or "Welcome home," but dat's Miss Susie for you always thinking about herself. Massa Taylor stepped out the wagon; he looked like he gained some weight, which he ain't need to do. His face looked even redder, his beard was overgrown, and he smelled much lak the horses. He reached out to kiss Miss Susie, but she turned her head, so he just planted a sweaty kiss on her cheek. She wiped off her face when he bent down to kiss her hand. Then Massa shouted, "Abraham, come unload the wagon!"

Miss Susie spoke up, "Abraham too old. Got another nigger to take his place;" she shouted "George!" He stepped out from the side of the house.

Massa slowly looked him up and down. "Well, looks like you been keeping up with your training. That's good, because I got some fights lined up for you. Okay, George, start unloading these vittles; they going bad by the minute." Then he yelled to the overseer "Get this nigger some better-fitting clothes he showing off everything he got."

I had laid out a fine spread of smoked ham, fried chicken, black-eyed peas, okra, collards, rice, all kinds of desserts, and of course, my delicious buttermilk biscuits. Massa loves my biscuits. The peach pie Miss Susie had me cook was still bubbling in the window, cooling off. I know Massa lak fresh strawberries, so I picked some from the garden and fixed a big bowl of sweet cream to go with 'em. Everybody ate real hearty, and afterwards, they all sang my praises 'bout what a great meal it was, dat made me feel good.

Since Massa been back, I see George even less. He been carrying him round to fight other niggers; I just pray he don't get hurt. I hear dese fights to the death can get quite brutal. They say the niggers do anything to win, like gouge each other eyes out and bite neck veins. I can't even picture such a cruel scene. All a sudden, I hear a lotta ruckus coming from the yard. Massa back and everybody was running toward him.

The wagon pulled up, I craned my neck to get a closer look. A body was laid out in the back of the wagon. Is dat George? But nobody answered me; my heart dropped. Is he dead? The overseer went round and started kicking at the still body.

"Git up, nigger. Git up!"

He slowly stirred, and when he raised his head, his face was so bloody I could hardly make out who he was, but I know that body and could tell it was George. Massa ordered the overseer to douse him with water. George roused a bit; then out of nowhere, the slaves started shouting "Big George, Big George!"

Slowly, he pulled himself up to his feet and raised his arms like a hero. Massa grabbed one of his arms and shouted "Big George is undefeated! He's the heartiest nigger round these parts; he ain't lost not one fight!" Massa was boasting 'bout his prized nigger buck. George was showing off, but he looked in bad shape.

I want so bad to touch him, but I can't get close enough. They took him to the barn to rest up. As I turned to leave, I looked up and saw Miss Susie standing in the window taking it all in. She looked worried too, but when she catch me looking at her, she snatched the curtains close. Later, I took George some food, when I opened the barn door, the sun streamed in and shined on his badly beaten body. He was lying on a pile of hay near the horse stall. As I moved closer, he raised his head, looked at me, and slightly smiled through bloody and swollen lips. His face looked like a piece of raw meat; he had deep scratches round his neck and lots of scrapes and bruises all over his body. I rubbed the top of his head; dat was 'bout the only place he ain't have no scars. I slowly fed him some porridge, which he ate a little at a time. We didn't speak; we just looked in each other's eyes; they did all the talking for us.

Massa Taylor took off again; he said for a short time, but we never know. That ain't stop Miss Susie from calling for George though. She called for him so much the overseer started to fuss, telling her he can't keep up with his training. Miss Susie ain't care; she told him to take care of the field slaves and she take care of the house slaves and dat was dat. Seem like something always wrong in Miss Susie bedroom, but I don't ever see where he be moving no furniture or making no repairs. Everything looks the same to me after he leaves. When I ask him what he be doing up there all the time, he don't pay me no never mind and start talking about sumptin' else. Whenever George hears her call his name, he gets a sick look on his face; you could tell he don't wanna go to her, but I tell him he has to; if not, he get in trouble. He goes, but I could tell his heart ain't in it, and dat makes me feel a little better 'bout this peculiar relationship.

Just Like Old Times

I ain't been feeling myself lately, but I keep pushing on; don't have no choice; gotta keep up with my endless duties. My stomach always upset, and I can't keep nuttin' down. Soon as I take food in, it come right back up. 'Bout all I can keep down is soda crackers and warm lemon water. I said to one of the slave girls "I don't know what I got, but I sho' be glad when it pass."

"Hmmph, dat so," she said. "Well, just know it may not pass for anudder eight months."

I spun my head around to her "What you talking 'bout?"

"You probably loaded."

"What you mean?"

"I mean you gonna have a baby dat's what!"

"Shut yo' mouth!" Then I think to myself, I could be 'specting, given the way me and George be going at it all the time. Every chance we get, we sneak away. We do it in the barn, upside the house, behind the firewood, down by the creek, anywhere we could. There ain't a place nearby we ain't sneak a piece, *hee, hee.*

Massa been back for some time now, and he been staying in Miss Susie room much more; guess he finally growed on her. Miss Susie seemed to be slowing down lately and sleeping in a lot mo'. She also keep asking me to fix her up strange foods lak strawberry jam with smoked fish on soda crackers. I never hear of such foods together. She looks like she picked up some weight too, but I ain't one to talk, cuz I did too. Soon, they announce dat Miss Susie was 'specting in the fall. All the slaves send up cheers when they hear a new white baby was coming. Dat kinda news always brings high spirits to a plantation, cuz when a slave owners' family growing, they tend to keep the slaves they got, may purchase new ones. Slaves have a better chance of keeping they own families together, but we ever know for sure. White folks do what they want; we never have no say what might happen to us or our families. I come to recognize dat I'se wid child too, and I'm happy 'bout it. I'm seventeen years old and this be my first child. Most slave girls be working on their second or third child by the time they fifteen.

Funny how me and Miss Susie keep doing the same thing together again just like when we was chillun. We rekindled our close relationship. She stays up under me all the time and keep asking me if I feel dis way or dat. She delights in sizing up our growing bellies, trying to figger out who's the biggest. Sometimes, I be trying to do my work, but she keep getting in my way, and I forced to work round her as she keeps babbling on 'bout much a nuttin'. Big George and I still steal away whenever we get a chance. We lay out amongst the field flowers while he rubs my back and belly; we talk 'bout getting a cabin together.

47

I would love nuttin' mo' than to share a cabin with George and our baby maybe even git married and jump the broom if we 'llowed too. But I don't know how Miss Susie would take to dat; she used to having me round the Big House all the time so I 'cided to wait til' after the baby come befo' I mention it. George said he glad Miss Susie with child, cuz she don't call for him no mo'.

We both know what was going on, but don't dare speak of it for fear of being overheard. If what happened ever comes out, no telling what might happen. For sho', George be a goner, but far as Miss Susie Lawd only knows. George ain't talk 'bout it in a long time, but he starts talking 'bout being free again.

He said "After the baby come, we gonna run away."

"Stop dat fool talk," I told him. "Ain't no point in talking 'bout being free. It ain't gonna happen."

For the first time, George got real mad with me. He jumped up. "Yes it can and it will. I may not be able to go back to Africa, but I be damn if I'se gonna be a slave the rest of my life, and I ain't gonna let my baby be no slave forevah. You do what you want, but I swear one day, you gonna look up and we both be gone. Dat's wid you or widout you."

That skeers me, cuz I know he mean it. The thought of losing George and our baby is too much to think 'bout, so I start talking 'bout sumptin' else "Massa ain't fighting you much lately. Dat mean you done?"

"Naw, he jest having a hard time finding anudder nigger to put up against me. White men ain't willing to set no wagers 'gainst me no mo', but knowing him, he hab me back out there soon enuff."

I was working in the kitchen one day when I start to feel wet. I looked down and saw I was standing in a puddle of water Thought I musta spilled some water, and jest keep on working. Then all of sudden, I got a terrible pain in my belly; it was so hard it bent me over.

A young slave gal said to me, "Lucy, yo' water broke. You 'bout to have yo' baby." She took me to a back room, laid me down, and ran to get the mammy that births the nigger babies. I was so skeered. I wanted my mammy, but she too far away, so I tell 'em to go fetch George. By now, erbody know 'bout us, so it don't matter. The pains keep coming and they getting' stronger; I let out a groan. Outta nowhere Miss Susie showed up and start asking:

"Lucy, is your baby coming? I thought my baby was coming first."

I ain't in no mood for Miss Susie's fool questions rat now; I jest want these pains to stop. The mammy start pressing on my stomach, then had me moved over to the birthing stool, where two slave women held my legs apart as the mammy kept pressing my belly to help push the baby come out; after a few good pushes, my baby come out screaming.

"It's a boy!" they all yelled.

Soon, George come running in and dropped down on the floor beside me. He looked at me and our son with pride, as we both listened to our son's healthy cries. He said "He sho got good lungs, don't he?"

I just smiled and turned my head. I was 'bout to drift off to sleep when I see Miss Susie standing in the doorway. Can't tell if she happy for me or sad for herself dat my baby come first. I can never figger that woman out.

Later that same night, Miss Susie let out the worse scream I ever hear in my life; sound like somebody was trying to kill her. The mammy ran to her, but she ain't 'llowed to touch no white woman. "Run git the doctor" she shouted. "Miss Susie baby coming."

The white doctor all the way in town, by the time they reach him, it may be too late. Miss Susie was screaming even louder now, and all the slaves come running up from slave row and standing round the Big House trying to figger out what was going on. Nobody seems to know what to do, but somebody betta do sumptin' and do it quick. Miss Susie was screaming for mercy.

"Please, somebody, anybody, come help me. I'm dying." Then all of a sudden, it got real quiet and stayed quiet for a long time. I listened for the baby's cry, but I ain't hear nuttin'. Erybody looks worried but don't nobody say nuttin'.

I asked one of the slave girls as she passed by "What's going on?"

She said, "Miss Susie baby come, but it come out dead."

Oh my God! What a shame! Po' Miss Susie. I feel so sorry for her; she must be so sad and Massa ain't even here to comfort her. Wish I could go see 'bout her, but I can hardly move. The mammy who was with Miss Susie when her baby came out appeared at my door, and she was holding a blanket in her arms. She ain't say nuttin'; she just came in and kneeled down next to me. Then she pulled the blanket back, and what I seen almost took my breath away. It was a dead baby, a dead black baby. Ain't no doubt it was black; it had a black-shaped nose and the ears and fingertips was dark. I just looked at the poor dead baby; it was a boy baby too. I prayed softly "May God rest his po' little soul."

I looked up at the mammy and she had a strange look on her face. She said to me "Lucy, I come for yo' baby. Miss Susie wanna see yo' baby."

"No, not now; my baby still feeding and pulled my baby closer to my breast. "She can't see him just yet. I take him to her later."

The mammy slowly wrapped the dead baby back up and handed it to anudder slave woman standing next to her. Then she went to reach for my baby, but I pushed her hands away. "No!" I said She looked at me real stern, then grabbed hold of my arms and held me down.

Somebody reached over and put a cloth over my nose; that was the last thing I remember. I don't know how long I was out, but when I come to, I had the most awful headache and a strange odor was lingering in the air. Smelled like laudanum, medicine the doctor use to knock folks out befo' he pulls teeth or cut off a limb. I start to feel round for my baby, but I can't find him. I pulled back the covers and looked all round for him. Where is he? Then it came to me what was going on befo' I fell off to sleep. I started screaming "Where's my baby? Where's my baby?"

George came rushing in, threw his body on top of me and was holding me down. I tried to push him off, but he was too heavy. "Gimme my baby!" I cried. "Where's my baby?" He said sumptin', but I can't make out what he said. "What you say?"

"He gone!"

"Gone? What you mean he gone?"

"He dead!"

"What? Can't be, he fine. I held him in my arms. He was suckling at my breasts. He can't be dead. Miss Susie's baby dead, but my baby fine. Gimme my baby. I want my baby now!", I screamed. I felt like I was losing my mind. I ain't wanna hear nuttin' from nobody. I jest want my baby. I ain't sho' what happened, but I musta fainted away again. When I woke back up, I was dizzy and weak. I was all alone; I struggled to my feet, as my head was spinning round. I grabbed hold to the wall for support and made it to the door. I looked round, but I ain't see nobody. Where is everybody? I wondered. I struggled to get to the back stairwell and started crawling up the steps but had to stop every few feet to gain my strength. When I got to Miss Susie's bedroom door, I used my last bit of strength to kick it open. She was laying in bed, staring out the window. Barely able to speak, I said "Where my baby, Miss Susie?"

She turned her head and looked at me, then turned back and began staring out the window. Again I said, "Where my baby, Miss Susie?"

She slowly turned back around and stared at me with the most hateful look on her face. Then she said to me *"My baby died. Your baby had to die too. Wouldn't be right for you to have something I ain't have, now would it?"*

"What! What you say?" I couldn't believe my ears. What she talking 'bout? Rage took over me, and befo' I knew it, I was on top of that bitch trying to strangle the life out of her. I was like a mad woman; it ain't matter to me dat I was a slave and she was my mistress. I jest wanted to kill her. Somebody was pulling me away, but I kept grabbing at her, trying to git a better hold of her.

She yelled out "Come get this nigger girl off me! She done lost her mind!"

"You damn right!" I jumped back on her and tightened my grip around her neck. George came and snatched me up, he put me under his arms, and carried me down the steps as I keep kicking and screaming. He tried to calm me down, but nuttin' could at that point. One minute, I wanted to kill Miss Susie, and the next, I wanna kill myself so I could be with my baby. I can't take this life no mo'; too much suffering.

Life Goes On

Life went on at the Taylor Plantation, but not for me and it never will. It's been a year since my baby passed. My life been changed forever. I won't ever be able to get over my baby's death. I ain't even git a chance to name him before he was taken from me. I never had nuttin I could call my own; dat baby would have been the first. He gave me a reason to go on; now don't nuttin matter no mo' to me. That baby was a part of me and George, the only man I ever loved. Lawd, what have I done to warrant this life? I'm a good person and a good slave, but I'm tired. I can't live like this no mo'! I swear, as God is my witness, I'm gonna make Miss Susie pay for what she did, if it takes the rest of my life.

Several weeks later, Miss Susie announced her family was coming for a visit. I was so happy to hear dat cuz dat's the plantation I grew up on and where my mammy still lives. I can get to see my mammy. I miss her so much; only seen her once in two years and not at all since my baby died. I can't wait to see her; I need to lay my head on her caring bosom and feel her comforting arms around me. She been through much more than me and for a longer time; she help me feel better.

I go about fixing a big meal; cooking has a way of easing my mind. I also want to make my mammy proud, so she knows all her lessons ain't go to waste. I was still cooking when I looked out and saw wagons turn in and start up the long, winding, dusty road toward the Big House. My heart started beating fast; I snatched off my apron and ran out. I nervously waited for the two wagons to pull up. The lead wagon will hold Miss Susie's ma and pa, and the second wagon will hold the servants; my mammy most likely be in dat one. I watched as a nigger coachman jumped down, opened the door of the lead wagon, and helped the Taylors step out. Miss Susie ran up to greet her folks, and they commence to hugging, smiling, and crying happy tears. I was looking to see my mammy step out the udder wagon, but some udder slave women come out; two older ones and a young girl.

I couldn't wait no mo', so I ran up to one of the slave women and asked her "Where's my mammy?"

"Who yo' mammy?"

"What you mean, who my mammy? The head mammy, dat's who! Now where she at?"

Erybody was looking at me.

Then Miss Susie's mother spoke up "Lucy, your mammy is sick, so we decided it was best to leave her home to rest up."

"What's wrong with her?"

"I don't know, just that she was too sick to travel, but she told me to tell you she loves you and will see you soon. I wouldn't worry. I'm sure she'll be fine." Then, they all went back to hugging and kissing like nuttin happened, when my world had shifted yet again. I just stood there with tears streaming down my face.

Lawd, what I gonna do now? I ain't got no baby, no mammy, I ain't got nuttin; I ain't even got myself. I ran back to the kitchen, dropped to my knees, and just cried. I was still crying when the same slave woman I spoke to earlier came in.

She reached down, pulled me to my feet, and wrapped her arms around me. I just melted away. I wept and I wept some mo' as she held me close to her bosom, jest like my mammy woulda done.

She told me "Chile, I know you suffering rat now, but yo' mammy told me to tell you to be strong. You be all right. You can handle this and whatever else comes yo' way, cuz God is on your side. He will protect you. You must believe dat." She went on to tell me my mammy's health been failing for some time now and that she old, tired, and her body can't hold up like it used to. "But you still young and strong. You got a lot of life ahead of you. You got a chance to make the best of your life. You can't give up." Her words touched my heart and lifted my spirit. It was like my mammy was standing there talking to me herself. She was right; I can't give up and I won't; I'm gonna start to live my life the best I can, and I now know dat being a slave ain't my best. From now on, I'm gonna live like I ain't got many mo' days to be a slave. A short time later, they told me my mammy died; I prayed for God to give her eternal rest and everlasting peace.

The War

It's 1862 and a war's been raging between the North and the South for over a year. The South fighting to keep slavery going, and the North trying to stop it, but the South seem to be losing. White folks running round like chickens with they heads cut off; skeered they gonna lose erything, 'specially the slaves, which is a big part of how they able to get by. They hell bent on keeping us slaves forever. Massa keep many newspapers in his library, and I glance through them when no one's round; they all say the war was getting worse and dat the South is losing a lot of men. Don't seem to matter much to Massa Taylor though; he still keep talking about taking George round to fight. By now, Miss Susie had grown tired of hearing him talk 'bout dat; she real nervous about the war.

I hear her tell him "The North is threatening the Southern way of life. They gonna free the slaves and change everything if we don't fight back." She screamed at him "Instead of talking about fighting George, you need to go fight in the war yourself! That's the only fighting I want to hear about from now on. Stop it and stop it now, you hear me?" They argue 'bout the war all the time.

Massa Taylor don't seem at all moved by her words, or the war for that matter; it's lak he in a world all his own. He won't never no brave man been a slacker most his life. All he ever do is go round and spend his daddy money. Erything he got is cuz his daddy give it to him and cuz he a white man nuttin' else. His family may have wealth, but he ain't do nuttin' to add to it; fars as I could tell.

Massa keep carrying on 'bout getting fights lined up for George, said he plans to take him to Maryland to get some wagers on him. George keep training but said he don't tend to fight no mo' and kill or maim no mo' colored men merely for the white man's musement. Said if he kill anybody, it'll be one of dem and I know he mean it too. I now understand what George been saying all along; being a slave forever ain't something to settle for. Together, we start plotting our escape. Every chance we get, we put our heads together to plan the best way to get away. I was dusting Massa's library one afternoon, and spotted a map on his desk. For years, Massa been going on faraway treks and marked the different roads he traveled. Many of 'em was headed north; it appears he been as far north as Maryland, right up to the Masons and Dixon line; just on the other side is Pennsylvania. I remember George telling me 'bout states where slaves live free; he said Pennsylvania got plenty free slaves.

He also tell me 'bout a slave man who ran away from a nearby plantation but befo' he left said he was headed to Philadelphia, Pennsylvania, and he was never heard from again. They even send slave patrollers after him with 'special trained dogs called "nigger dogs"; they don't do nuttin but run down slaves; they half wolf and half hound; if they catch you, they been known to rip a slave apart if the patrollers don't get to 'em in time, but nobody seen hide nor hair of that runaway ever again. Most times, when a slave get caught, they bring him back to show udder slaves what will happen if they try to get away. They whip, castrate, even kill 'em; dat make you think twice, even three times 'bout running away. Freedom sumptin all slaves want, whether they act on it or not, but they still want it. Whippings and killings don't even stop 'em. George been beat plenty times; it ain't stop him and I ain't gonna let it stop me.

Me and George talk about running away all the time now, but we keep it to ourselves. We jest need a good plan one we keep to ourselves, cuz we don't know who to trust. Many a slave been caught befo' cuz udder slaves give 'em up. They may not wanna tell, but the threat of a whipping, make 'em tell erytime, so we don't tell nobody. There's been a lot of talk round slave row 'bout some slave woman in Maryland who run off, went North, and keeps coming back to free udder slaves. Hard to believe, but they swear by it! They said she takes slaves from eastern shore Maryland into Pennsylvania, where they can live free. Said her name is; Harriett. Dat's it; dat's our plan; we got to get to Maryland. Just the thought of freedom makes me yearn for it even more. Maryland is the place we need to get to; jest need to figger out how and when. We don't know how we gonna get there; but pray for God to lead us the way.

Every evening, Massa Taylor retires to his library. He's always looking over his map, trying to track routes to Maryland. I hear him curse out loud "Goddamn Yankees got all the roads blocked north, and the Feds got all the roads blocked south! How a man supposed to conduct his business around here?" He still don't seem a bit troubled 'bout the war at all or what could happen if the South lose. But what

I keep hearing most in my head is what Miss Susie said "The North is threatening the Southern way of life. They gonna 'free the slaves' and change everything if we don't fight back." The "free the slaves" part stayed with me. I know Massa likes his brandy, so I make sure to keep his decanter full. One night, he was sleep over his desk like he always do.

He ain't hear me come in, so I called to him from the door "Massa, can I get you anything?" He ain't answer, so I called out to him louder "Massa!"

Suddenly, he sat up, arms flailing, knocking over his sniffer and spilling brandy all over his desk. I jumped back and just watched him from afar. When he settled down, I said to him "Massa, you want me to clean that up?"

He was drunk; he staggered to his feet. "Yes, come clean this mess up," he said and stumbled out the room. I started wiping off his desk but quickly picked the map up out of the spilled brandy before it got too wet. I took and laid it out on the floor in front of the fireplace so it could dry out; I was careful not to put it too close to catch fire. When it dried out, I took it to George and we secretly looked it over together. George can't read, but he can count a little and had seen Massa's map plenty times befo' when he took him on his treks. He used his fingers to count the number of states between South Carolina where we at and Maryland it's just three, we feel we can make it. We know it's gonna be risky and take a while, but we mo' 'termined than ever to make it. The mo' we talk, the stronger our quest for freedom became. I quickly returned the map to Massa's office before he noticed it missing. I study that map every chance I get and commit the routes to memory. Massa office was the cleanest it ever been, cuz I always be in there.

But I always put everything back like I found it. I had a close call once when Miss Susie come walking in looking for Massa and catch me pouring over his desk. She asked me what I was doing; I quickly spotted Massa's spectacles on the desk, so I told her I was just reaching to clean them off. She looked at me kinda strange for a short time befo' she turned and went on her way. Phew!

The Beginning of the End

A year passed and there's a lot of unrest in the area. White folks running skeered, and the men keep meeting to plan ways to defend they plantations if the Union Army reaches them, tonight, they meeting here. I make it my bizness to be round to serve 'em so I can take in erything they say. I was pouring coffee when one of the men said "There is a real threat of raids on plantations located near the Combahee River."

Did he say Combahee River? That's rat where we is! I tried to keep calm, but my hands started to shake, and I spilled some hot coffee on the man's hand. He let out a loud yelp, and all the men turned to look at me. Massa Taylor was slouched over a chair in the back of the room fast asleep. He won't listening or watching nuttin' dat was going on. Somebody kicked his foot to wake him and told him what happened.

The man said to me "Git away from me, girl," as he wiped off his hand.

Massa sat up and shouted at me "Lucy, what you doing, girl?" I tried to speak, but no words would come out my mouth, *ah, ah.* He said "Get outta here."

He ain't gotta tell me twice I ain't want nuttin more den to get outta there. I turned and ran out as fast as I could. I need to find George so I can tell him what I heard.

Sometime in the middle of the night, a loud noise woke me up; it sounded like guns and I could smell gun smoke. I looked out the window and saw hoards of white Union soldiers riding up on horses and colored soldiers with guns running on foot; they was all headed toward the Big House. Then it came to me.

"Oh my God, we being raided!" Slaves was running all over the place screaming and crying, but not out of fear; they was cheering on the soldiers. George and udder slave men kicked in the front door of the house and came running in. I hear Miss Susie screaming to high heaven, then I see Massa Taylor. Some white soldiers had him gripped up by his collar; he was shaking and crying like a baby.

"Take what you want." He pulled his pockets inside out. "Here's some currency. Take the silver, furniture, whatever you want. Take my wife even." Miss Susie started cussing at him and calling him every name in the book. I couldn't hold back and laughed out loud; it was the funniest thing I ever seen.

The soldiers started ransacking the house, taking food, supplies, anything they could get their hands on with help from George and the udder men. The soldiers gave 'em guns, which they quick to use. Slaves that cried out for Massa or Miss Susie, they shot 'em down, men and women alike.

George said, "Dem niggers always gonna be slaves, free or not, so they better off dead." He wasn't playing; he meant bizness! Then he started looking around for that cracker overseer who ain't been seen since the fighting started. George shouted "Where you at, Cracker? Know you round here somewhere. Come show your cracker face." He motioned for some the men to spread out to look for him. Befo' long, we heard a holler; they found him, and he was begging for mercy.

All the young girls and boys he had raped for years was screaming "Kill 'em! Kill 'em!"

The men threw a rope over a nearby tree and put him on a horse, they tied his hands behind his back, put a noose round his neck and hit the horse; dat cracker, redneck rose up twitching round like a slaughtered pig.

They brought Massa Taylor and Miss Susie out on the porch; they was looking around, wild-eyed.

One of the colored soldiers said, "Listen, we're here to make sure nothing is left for the Confederates.

What you do with them is your business. You handle them as you see fit."

Massa and Miss Susie started screaming and crying again; I couldn't tell who was screaming the loudest. Miss Susie mouff was wide open; I walked over and spat right in it. She was utterly stunned. I screamed at her "Hush Up!" "How it feel to be so helpless?

Now you know how I was when you killed my baby! But you ain't care 'bout me, did you? For long as I knowed you, you ain't never care 'bout nobody but yo'self. You the most selfish piece of flesh and blood I ever laid eyes on." Then I reared back and slapped her crossed her face as hard as I could, then slapped her cross her other cheek and she fell to the floor.

She just sat there looking up at me, whimpering and holding her face. She looked like she was 'bout to say sumptin', but I stopped her. I pointed to her and said; "You ain't got nuttin to say to me ever again I never want to hear your voice or see your wicked face ever again." Then I turned and walked away; I was done with Miss Susie forever.

The Union commander told us they had steamboats on the riverbanks waiting to take us north. We screamed with joy and happiness. Then he told us "You can thank one of your own for your freedom. A slave woman turned scout for the Union Army gave us the information that we used to get through Confederate lines. Her name is Harriet; Harriet Tubman."

George and I looked at each other and smiled; dat has to be the same Harriet we heard about, the one we planned to find, but she found us first. Praise God! Maybe one day we git to thank her. We gathered up our belongings, picked up the small children, and started walking toward the riverbanks with the colored soldiers guiding our way, but our men stayed behind. As we walked, we heard a big blast and saw a huge plume of flames coming from the Taylor Plantation. It was on fire! We stopped to watch all the misery and suffering that had lasted for decades and everything that came with it go up in smoke. The men came riding over the horizon, shouting and shooting their guns up in the air. Big George; I mean Eqquos, was leading the way. The freedom he always believed we would have one day has finally come. Me and my African king is finally free. Hallelujah!

The End

Chapter 3
What's Freedom?

NATCHEZ, MISSISSIPPI, 1867

Beulah

Beulah the name they give me, so that's what I call myself. I still young, but I done seen a lot in my few years, including the Civil War. The war been over 'bout two years now; they say we free, but life ain't get no better for us; it get even worse. We may look happy on the outside, but inside, most slaves don't know what free even mean. Free to do what? Free to go where? Saying you free and being free two different things. I been a slave all my life, and white folks been telling me what to do and when to do it as far back as I can remember. Now that I'se free, I can do what I want, just don't know how. Some slaves followed the Union troops north, but others like me stayed behind. When they first tell me I'se free and white folks don't own me no mo', I act like I know what they was saying, but I ain't really know; not really. But when I hear 'em say, "From now on, if whites wanna keep you on, they have to pay you for your labor." That stuck in my head, so I 'cided to stay put. After all, I know my way round here and know what needs to be done, cuz I been doing it all my life, so why leave? I figger if I can get paid for my labor, I can care for my own self and my family, but that ain't what happened; least not so far. So I keep on doing what I been doing, but if I ain't a slave no mo', why I still feel like one and why do whites still treat me like one?

But I'se getting restless now; time I find out what freedom is, what it look like, what it feel like, and what I'm s'posed to do with it. Free slaves don't know how to be free and slave owners don't know what to do with free slaves; dese some troubling times for both. The South lost much more than the war; many white men died and the ones that come back had awful wounds and missing limbs. Before the Union armies left, they raided the plantations, took everything in sight, and destroyed what was left. They burned up most of the fields and left much of the South in shambles. I heard a plantation owner say "It's gonna take time for things to return to normal," but normal ain't normal no mo'. White folks real bitter 'bout losing the war; they hate the North, but seem like they hate us mo' and makes life even harder for us.

They lay all the blame for their suffering on us slaves, when they the ones at fault for keeping us slaves. You can't keep people down for hundreds of years, turn round, and say you free and 'spect them to just move on and ack like nuttin' ever happened, cuz it did. Slavery caused so much hurt and sorrow and the pain runs too deep for us to just pick up, dust ourselves off, and get over it. Even though we s'posed to be free, whites still treat us like we slaves, many flat out tell us, "We ain't paying you niggers nuttin' no matter what the gubmint says."

When a slave dare ask to be paid or tempt to leave, they beat 'em real bad, even hang some, so where that leave us? We as helpless as babes in the woods! Whites still use fear to keep us in our place, so it don't matter; free or slave, we'se right back where we started. Ain't nuttin' change; so most fall back into they slave ways, cuz that's all we know. Slavery been goin' on fo' hundreds of years, and from the looks of it, it may take anudder hundred for freedom to take hold.

Scores of ex-slaves roam the southlands like lost souls, searching mostly in vain for family who was sold away, hoping to bring their families back together again. Thousands of colored families been ruined, had everything took away freedom of movement, freedom to learn, freedom to marry, freedom to just be! They took away our religion, culture, and cut off our history. They even took away our given names and call us what they want, when they ain't calling us *niggers*. The killings, beatings, and selling away our families has left lasting scars not only on our bodies, but on our souls, as well as our minds. There's been too much suffering, but we strong. Wouldn't be no more of us left if we won't and we prideful too. I'se an American slave, born and raised rat here in America, so was my mammy and pappy. But I remember my pappy telling me stories about the people who come befo' us; he said they was even stronger than we is. He told me how many years ago, the white man stole Afrikins, brought 'em cross the waters in chains, made 'em slaves, and keep us all that way for years on end. He said they the ones we come from, so I know we strong. Ain't many old Afrikins left; can't even remember the last time I saw one. When they all gone, won't nobody be round to tell they story, I make sho' to tell my children, so they can tell they children and hope they pass it on. If not, we won't have no recollection at all of our Afrikin peoples and dat would be a terrible shame.

The lives of former slaves and former slave owners changed a lot since the war ended, and for colored women and white women, the change went even further. We round each other most times, and the white mistress have say over all her female slaves and oversees everything we do, not just the female house slaves. She even calls in female field hands, when they needed. Use 'em as milk maids or bring 'em in the house for extra help. We have the babies and whites want us to keep having babies, so they have a never-ending supply of slaves. We don't even own our wombs. Ain't nuttin' worse than having your child ripped out your arms like it was never part of you after you done carried it in your own belly. I tell you, it's the most painful thang a slave woman will ever face and one she will carry in her soul the rest of her life.

I been with Miss Blair's family most my life; I first belonged to anudder one of her family members, who sold me to them to settle a debt, I was told. I was about ten years old and never seen my mammy, pappy, brothers, or sisters ever again. Never will forget that terrible day; I cried maself to sleep every night for years. I still don't know what ever come of my family. I spend most my days serving Miss Blair's every need. I cook, clean, wash her clothes, even wash her too, scrubbing her back every time I draw her bath. I all but raised her only child too; Miss Sara; I been caring for her since she came in the world. She must be 'bout twelve years old now. She smart, tender-hearted and much warmer than her cold momma. Never even seen Miss Blair hug her child or spend any real time with her.

Even so, I believe Miss Sara will grow up to be a fine young woman; kinda sorry I won't be round to see her all growed up, but time I think 'bout my own children now.

Miss Blair ain't close to none of her slaves, but befo' the war, she seemed to favor me most. She knew she can always 'pend on me; I know what she wants even before she know she wants it. I waited on that woman hand and foot and was the best slave she ever had. I took care of her day after day, night after night, no matter what; it never mattered what I wanted, never mattered what any slave wanted. What always mattered was what white folks wanted, and that was everything we had to give then they wanted even more. Many of the wealthy white ladies had lost they husbands in the war. They was used to living in the lap of luxury befo' the war, but now, they left alone to keep up they plantations. With not much money left and most of their property gone, they feel helpless and 'shamed of their new class, and class is very important to rich white folks. They don't just look down on niggers; they look down on poor whites too; mostly Irish whites. Rich whites call 'em "white trash" saying "The Irish ain't nuttin' more than niggers turned inside out."

They use 'em as servants and they do much the same work as niggers do, often side by side us, but they don't git treated near as harsh as we do. The Irish women work right long side us and we bond, but many the Irish men hate the idea of being treated lak niggers and be mean and disagreeable with us. Dat's why many plantation owners have 'em oversee us, knowing they keep nigger slaves in line. The Irish know they ain't thought of much better than niggers, but in the eyes of rich white folks they white skin, make 'em better den us.

Miss Blair been real sullen and angry lately; most the time she ack lak I ain't even round; don't pay me no attention at all. Barely looks my way and hardly parts her lips when I ask her something; she just motion and shake her head yes or no. Other slave women tell me they white mistresses been treating them the same way, even the ones that used to be kind. But now they downright cruel; some even strike their slave women for the slightest thing.

Many say they mistress treat 'em cold and act like they don't want 'em round no more, but still 'cept our free labor and that's 'xactly how Miss Blair's been treating me. Seem like she don't care if I come or go, so I 'cide to come right out and ask her. Even though they tell me I don't need her say so no mo', it's taking me time to get used to that. I don't wanna jes up and leave; I need to speak with her first but no matter what she say I still plan to leave here. Mississippi holds too many bad memories for me to stay here any longer. I'm tired of living like a slave and knowing I'se free, even if I don't know what it means. But first, I wanna talk with Miss Blair; that's if she lets me. I find her sitting on the porch drinking the iced tea I sat out for her earlier; she ain't ask me for it, I just know she likes her tea round the same time every day; just can't seem to break my slave habits.

Befo' I stepped out on the porch, I stood back and studied her, trying to see what kinda mood she in. She looks sorrowful and deep in thought; I kinda feel sorry for her now that she a widow. I know she ain't used to fending for herself and taking charge of things her husband used to look after. Her husband wasn't killed in the war, but he got hurt real bad and lost both his legs. He lingered for almost a year before he died, and ever since then, she's been real low and growing more bitter by the day. She tries to keep up a good face when she round other white ladies, but they all seem troubled. Don't know why my mind keeps wandering back to white folks; I sho' need to break that habit. From here on out, I'm gonna keep my mind on my own problems. I gathered up my nerve and started thinking 'bout what I was gonna say to Miss Blair.

I want her to know I'se grateful for the years she took care of me and my family, but I also want her to know I ain't never ask to be taken care of in the first place no more than I asked to be a slave; none of the other thousand of slaves asked to be either. I have no idea what might be headed my way, but I know it can't be no worse than what I'm 'bout to leave behind. I musta surprised Miss Blair, cuz when I come up from behind her, she jumped, but soon as she seen it was me, she sat upright.

She said crossly "What do you want, Beulah?"

Hmm, that's the first time she uttered any words to me in weeks. I ain't want to rile her, so I kept my voice low.

"Miss Blair, I don't mean to bother you, ma'am. I just wanna know if you want me to stay or leave, cuz of late, it don't seem lak you want me round no mo', and if you don't ..." Before I could even finish what I was 'bout to say, she held up her hand and stopped me.

She got up from her chair and started coming toward me. First, I thought she was gonna hit me, so I reared back. Then she got right in my face, pointed her finger and let out a rant lak I never heard befo'.

"You black niggers have caused me more trouble than your worth. Seems like ever since those damn Yankees stole the war from us and changed everything we know to be right, you slaves do nothing but show your ungratefulness by running away or demanding to be paid for the work you've been doing all your worthless lives. What about the years we took care of you and your families? You dumb niggers don't know the first thing about taking care of yourselves. How long you think you can last without white people doing for you?"

I tried to speak but she started right up again. "What makes you think a poor, ignorant nigger woman like you can fend for yourself, much less care for your ugly, nappy headed pickannies? You owe me everything you got. I been good to you niggers. Where you going? Don't nobody want you shiftless, lazy niggers." I just keep on looking at her as she spewed out her angry words and watched as her face grew beet red. Her mean words flew out of her mouth right along with the spit that was hitting me in the face, so I stepped aside to get out of her line of fire. Why she so angry with me? I wondered. What I ever do to her? I can't believe all the vile things she was saying to me. She took a short breath and was just 'bout to start up again.

Befo' I could help it, words came spilling out my mouff. "Miss Blair, everything you say we ain't got is cuz of you. Everything we don't know is cuz of you and other white folks like you. If we ignunt, it's cuz you won't let us learn, not cuz we caint. You took everything from us, but mostly, you took our freedom. What makes you think you had the right to take our freedom? I as human as you, bleed blood like you do, but you treat me and my people like we'se animals worse than you do animals. You starve us, beat us, rape us, kill us, and treat us like trash, then caste us off when you don't need us no more. Y'all keep us down for so long we don't even know how to treat each other. You white people fixed it so we hate ourselves, hate our own blackness. All my life, I had to put white folks' needs ahead of my own, but no mo'. At long last, I can put me and my family first, and I 'tend to do just that. I don't give a damn what you think 'bout me or how you feel 'bout me or my people. It may take some time to learn how to be free, but now that I is, I'm gonna live free and ain't nuttin' you can do 'bout it.

I may not know much, but I got good enough sense to know freedom has to be better than slavery ever was or ever will be. I'se free now and my days of asking you for anything is behind me forever. I'm leaving here and taking my life the life the good Lawd give us 'fo' you white people snatched it away, but God is good, cuz he done give it back. I don't owe you nuttin' not nuttin' at all! I ain't yo' slave no mo'!"

After I had my say, I turned round and left her standing there with her mouth hanging open, lak she was too dazed to speak. I ain't never in my life speak to Miss Blair or no other white person like that befo'; don't know what got into me. But what I do know now that I spoke my piece; I betta be gone and gone quick. As I was leaving, I could still hear her screaming after me.

"Go on! See if I care, you lazy nigger bitch! You'll be back. All you goddamn worthless slaves will be back. I know you will.

I don't pay no attention to her empty words and just kept on walking as fast as I could. I was shaking all over; tears was running down my face and I could feel rage just swelling up inside me. I can barely breathe, but I keep on walking, walking off to freedom land wherever dat is. I don't know what freedom looks like or feels like, I'm gonna step out on faith and let the Lawd lead me where I need to go. I'm ready to start a new life a free life.

We Leaving Here

I left the Blair Plantation that very day with just the clothes on my back and my three children in tow; my son Abraham, thirteen, my daughter, Noni, eleven, and my youngest son, Simon, nine. They all jumped when I came running in the run-down shack we had called home most our lives. I yelled at 'em "Gather up whatever you can carry, cuz we leaving." They looked like they was 'bout to ask me why, but before they could, I shouted "Don't ask me no nuttin'. Just pack up. We leaving here now, right now. Let's go!"

The Blair Plantation just a few miles outside of town, so we took off on foot walking as fast as we could. It was the middle of the day and the hot sun was high in the sky. We stopped at a creek along the way for a quick drink, then kept moving. I ain't sho' if Miss Blair sent somebody after me or not, but I can't take no chances. We kept walking as fast as our feet could carry us. By the time we reached the center of town, we was drenched, like somebody threw water on us. Town was bustling with huge numbers of colored people walking about, carrying all their worldly goods. Federal soldiers was everywhere keeping guard over us. Angry mobs of white folks, like the Klan, been going around beating and hanging colored men, even more than they was before we was free. They trying to scare us, and it's working, which why so many trying to leave here; it ain't safe for colored folks to be round here no more.

I spot a soldier sitting on a horse, and I run over to him. I asked him "Please, suh, can you help me? I wanna leave Mississippi and go north, anywhere north?" I don't think he heard me over all the noise, so I shouted louder, "I want to leave here. I want to leave here *now!*"

He looked down at me and said "Head on over to that building. They can help you," and he pointed me in the direction to go.

"Thank you, suh," I said and rushed off to where he directed me. When I got there, I saw hundreds of slaves milling around all trying to do the same as me; leave!

It was the Freedman's Bureau Field Office set up by the Union Army to help former slaves know they rights and to make sho' whites was following the laws they agreed to, but they ain't. A colored woman was passing by.

I stopped and asked her "I wanna leave here. What I need to do?"

"You ain't the first and won't be the last. We all trying to leave. You need to hitch yo'self a ride on a wagon, boat, train, anything leaving here."

"But I ain't got no money."

"Don't need none least not for now, but you better not wait much longer, or you may end up here forever. Head on over there and get in line."

After standing in line for hours, I finally made it to the front. There I saw a big desk with a Union soldier sitting on the other side.

He asked me "Where you coming from?"

I told him "The Blair Plantation, suh."

"How many in your family?" he asked me.

"Jes me and my three children," suh.

"Where you trying to get to?"

"Anywhere, suh, anywhere North, dat is."

"All you people want to go north. Don't know what makes you think thing's gonna be better for you there?"

"Please, suh, I ain't got no place else to go. I fear my mistress will kill me if I go back. I don't wanna be her slave no mo'. Please help me, please, I beg you."

Then a voice came from behind me, "I may be able to help you."

I turned around and saw an older white man with a uniform on, but it was different from the Union soldiers. I found out later he was a naval ship captain.

He looked at me and said, "I may be able to take you aboard my ship, if you willing to work. Can you cook and clean?"

"Oh yes, suh. I been cooking and cleaning all my life."

"Well, I could use a good cook and someone to keep the quarters clean."

"I can do that, suh, me and my children."

"Children, how many children you got?"

"Three, suh; two boys and a girl, and they all hard workers". Trained 'em all myself." I had left the boys outside to watch our belongings, and Noni was hiding behind my skirt.

He said, "I can use some hearty boys, but I don't have a need for no little girl," as he peered round me trying to get a better look at her. "Naw, I ain't got no need for her."

"Please, suh, I beg you. My daughter may be slight, but she strong and would be quite useful. You'll see. Please, suh. Please take me and all three my children."

The Union soldier behind the desk was looking on as we went back and forth. He broke in and said "Y'all need to step aside. I got lots more people to tend to; go handle your business elsewhere." We both left, but I closely followed the man outside, pleading with him every step of the way.

"Suh, please, I beg you. I don't care where you going, long as you going north."

"I'm headed to Ohio."

"Ohio? I never hear of dat place befo'. Is it north, suh?"

"About as north as you can get before you end up in Canada."

I kept after him. Ohio fine, suh; please take me and my children with you.

Finally he said "Okay, but understand this ain't no free ride. You and your children have to work hard to pay for your passage, and I can't have y'all eating up all the food rations. Barely got enough for my crew, you hear me?"

"Oh yes, suh!" Then I took his hand and kissed it. I was 'bout to thank him, "Suh—" but he stopped me.

"Call me Captain, Captain Evers."

"Yes, suh, Captain Evers. I promise I'll work harder than I did in my entire slave life, and I will be in your debt forever."

Captain Evers took us all aboard and commenced to telling us 'bout his big naval ship. He told us his ship don't carry passengers, just soldiers. His is a freight ship; he talked about how his ship transported goods and supplies to the Union soldiers during the war and crossed the Atlantic Ocean laying telegraph cable. He said his ship helped the North win the war, because President Lincoln used the telegraph to pass messages to his officers. He said he plans to take his ship to Europe after this trip was done.

New Life

My sons hung on every word of the stories the captain and his sailors was telling us about their many journeys. When we first set sail me and the children was kinda scared. We never seen so much water befo', and I don't even know how to swim. The ship was real rocky, and we kept falling down, but we soon got our sea legs, as they told us, and went right to work. The crew was former Union soldiers mostly white men and a few colored ones. From the start, the colored crewmen took my boys under their wings and began teaching them everything they needed to know about running a freight ship. I enjoy watching my sons learn new things and take so easily to this new life. The sailors let us know we was heading up the Mississippi River, through the Missouri, than follow the eastern routes toward the Ohio River. Along the way, we stopped at several ports, and each time, the captain sent me ashore to purchase food and provisions for the remainder of the trip. I always made a point of taking notice of the colored folks at each port; how they looked, how they dressed, and if they freely moved about. Whenever I got a chance, I always struck up conversations with some of the colored women. I asked them how different life was for them now that they free.

Most said freedom was hard, not nearly as hard as slavery, but just about. They tell me white folks still don't pay 'em like they s'posed to, and when they do, it usually ain't fair wages. They also overcharge them for food and rent making it even harder to get by. With white folks still in charge, they go out their way to make life even harder for colored folks. It's like they want to make our free lives just as bad, if not worse, than our slave lives was. They even made up new laws to keep former slaves down; called *Slave Codes* or *Black Codes*. One of the laws made it so they can pick up colored men for no reason, put 'em on chain gangs, and force 'em to work for free. It's the same as slavery, only they don't call it that, but it's just the same. I don't believe whites ever gonna do right by us, for fear they may have to share the wealth they earned from our fee labor for hundreds of years.

Me and Noni the only females on board; we do all the cooking, cleaning, and serving the captain and his crewmen round the clock. Caring for more than eighty-some crewmen was hard work. They keep us busy all the time working day and night.

Shortly after leaving shore Captain Evers started pestering me for sex. He warned me that if I refused him, he would drop us off at the next Southern port or might have us all thrown overboard. Oh, Jesus! I couldn't chance that; if that what it takes to get me and my children to a place where we can be safe and live free, then that's what I got to do. What choice do I have? The first time he took me he noticed the brand on the inside of my thigh and asked me how I got it. I told' him when I was just thirteen years old, the Massa who bought me kept me up in the Big House with him. He ain't have no wife; his nigger house mammy ruled everything. I was s'posed to be a chambermaid, but I never had much work to do, least not when he was round. She told me my job was to stay with Massa and keep him happy, so I did. She gave me clothes to wear, but they was for a much older girl, I could barely hold up the corset she give me. I just sat by him while he looked me over, telling me how pretty I was. He was always kind to me though, never raised a hand to me.

Every evening, he had me sit through dinner with him; said he liked my company. One night, as he stroked my hair, he asked me if I want to be his "conkbine." I was young and ain't know what that mean, but since he was always kind to me, I just said "Yessuh."

Later that night, he had one of his slave men come for me; he took me down to the barn, where two other slave men held me down. They forced my legs open and burned that mark on the inside my thigh. I screamed bloody murder; it hurt so bad. I found out later that massas who don't want no other men to touch his slave gal had her branded on the breast or thigh to show that she belongs to him only. That same night, he took me for the first time and almost every night after that. He the father of all three my children, and I was with him until he died years later. I was sold away again, but he willed that me and my children must always be sold together, and I'se so thankful for that.

Female slaves get taken all the time; that's why I keep Noni close to me. I tried as hard as I could to keep her safe and away from all the men folks on board, but I worry, cuz they so many of 'em. One night, as she was headed back to the galley six white sailors cornered her and gang-raped her. As soon as I heard her scream, I ran to her and started throwing men off her left and right; I fought 'em off one by one. I still don't know where I got the strength from; I was so angry I could have killed 'em all with my bare hands.

Seeing my baby girl all beat up and torn apart like that broke my heart, and to make matters worse it was her twelfth birthday. I cleaned her up and held her in my arms all night as we cried together. Noni was never right after that; she stayed sick the rest of the trip and got so weak she could hardly walk. Of course, my sons and the colored crewmen knew what happened, but they was forced to turn a blind eye. They know if they were to rise up, they would be killed; we might all be killed.

For years whites let colored men know they dare not stand up for their family, 'specially the females. At the same time, colored females learn not to depend on their menfolk. It's painful watching slave men forced to turn away as their wives and children get beaten and taken, often right in front of their eyes, with no way to help 'em. Slavery ain't jest take away a colored man's freedom; it also took away his very manhood and made him feel useless in every way. That mindset and forced separation may have destroyed colored families forever. We may be free, but long as our minds is controlled by whites, we will always be slaves. That's sad, but true!

Captain Evers keeps trying to talk me into staying on after we arrive in Ohio and go on with him to Europe. I don't plan to stay with him no longer than I have to, but I can't let him know that, cuz he might turn on me; then we all be in danger. Sex between white men and slave women been going on for as long as I know. Slave women often forced into using sex, jest so we can have some control over our lives and those of our children and even our men at times. If she refuses a white man, she apt to get beat and taken anyway, then sold herself or have her children sold away. White men blame his misdeeds on a slave woman's lustful ways, white wives get jealous and turn on the slave woman. They hit, kick, and treat her bad; some even been known to kill her and her children too if she think they was fathered by her husband. Don't nobody look after nigger women; we have to fend for ourselves. "White men may have power over our bodies, but they will never, ever be able to defeat a black woman's soul".

As we got close to Ohio, I sat my oldest son Abraham down and had a long talk with him. I watched him and could see him grow with his new learning. He told me he no longer felt like a slave, for the first time in his life, he felt free. This trip has given him a sense of pride and purpose. He dropped his head and shyly admitted he planned to stay on with the captain and his men when the ship leaves Ohio. I raised his head and looked in his eyes; I told him I understood his need for a better life, and I wanted the same for him. We prayed together for his safety, and I gave him my blessings. My younger son, Simon, wanted to stay behind too, but Abraham told him he needed to stay to take care of me and his sister but promised to come back someday and I believe he will.

Finally, we arrived in the port of Cincinnati, Ohio. I rejoiced and prayed that our free life in Ohio will be better than the slave life we left back in Mississippi. But my joy ain't last long; when Noni was attacked, she got pregnant. I 'spected she was and did all I could to help her, but her health just kept failing. We wasn't there a month before she died giving an early birth; she was just too young and too frail. As much as I mourned her death, I almost welcomed it, because she was in no more pain. I took pride knowing both she and her baby died free; they the first in our family to die free. Now they can live in heaven, free forever.

Life in Ohio

After we arrived in Ohio, Captain Evers surprised me with a generous amount of money. He apologized for what happened to Noni, thanked me for my hard work, and wished me well. I was grateful for his kindness and goodwill. I used that money to pay for a meager room and to purchase some food to hold me and Simon over until I could find work. They told me during slavery, hundreds of slaves escaped to Canada through Ohio along the Underground Railroad. I sure wish I'd known that sooner, because Canada is where Captain Evers' ship was headed when he left here. I pray my son Abraham stays there so we can meet up again one day.

Things are much different here in Ohio, as I hoped it would be. The first thing I saw was a large number of free colored people living here. They dressed well, move about freely, and many of 'em was educated too. They even got schools for colored children, with both white and colored teachers; I never thought I'd see that. They told me President Abraham Lincoln the same white man who freed us, passed a law that said "All colored people have full citizenship of the United States, with all protections under the law," just like white folks; *I added that part.*

Times are changing, but I don't let myself get use to the changes. Whites have a way of going back on their word and taking things back, 'specially if it look like we getting ahead. If they have their way, we be held back forever free or not.

It ain't take me much time to find work as a housekeeper for a well-to-do white family. They kind folks and treat me well told me they was abolitionists and helped free many slaves. But most of all, they pay me fair wages, and that's a blessing in itself. Being able to be a wage earner so I can take care of me and my child is the best feeling I ever had in my life. In my off hours, I take in laundry; I'm used to working hard. That ain't nothing new to me. What is new was getting paid for my labor; I'm still trying to get used to that. I set aside my extra earnings so I can buy us a house. I worked day and night until I earned enough to buy a small house in the black section of town; it ain't much, but its mine and I'm proud of it. It feels so good to be able to do things on my own, with no help or say-so from white folks.

My son Simon found several odd jobs around town; white folks took notice of how sharp he was and how fast he caught on; he's a real smart boy. A white teacher name Miss Kincaid opened a school for colored children and asked if he wanted to come to her school. I remember the day he came running home to ask me, but befo' he could finish asking me, I said "Course you can, boy. You go and learn as much as you can." Just knowing my child gonna be able to learn to read and write is such a gratifying feeling.

Many of the colored children have to walk miles to school, rain or shine, but they don't miss a day. The school building is falling down around 'em, the roof leaks when it rains, and they just have an old wood stove to keep 'em warm in the winter. They ain't got many books, but none of that stops them from wanting to learn, not at all. Miss Kincaid told me the children can hardly wait to come to school and don't even want to stop at the end of the day; they just wanna keep on learning. How uplifting that was to hear. I always knew if we was given a chance to learn, we could and we would. Seeing former slave children so eager to learn is a wonderful sight. But some of the colored parents don't let they children attend school; said they need 'em to work and earn money for the family. I don't understand that cuz we free now and allowed to learn. I feel 'specially bad for the girls; they smart and real keen on learning even more than some of the boys, but they folks don't see no value in teaching girls. How sad. My Simon did so good in school dat Miss Kincaid let him teach the younger children, and he teach me too. I learned how to count the coins I earned and how to read some words in the Bible. Life getting better; I'm beginning to feel free.

The Return of Miss Blair

Five years passed and Simon a full-fledged teacher now and he loves teaching. He keep telling me 'bout some new white teacher who just arrived here from Mississippi, who he was eager for me to meet. I told him I'll get round to meeting her, but I'm too busy right now. Then one day, he came running home to tell me the new teacher said he won't be able to teach no more if I don't come to the school right away. She told him she was gonna kick him out of school.

"Over my dead body," I quickly said. I dropped everything and headed over to the school house to deal with that new teacher. "Who she think she is?" I grumbled to myself as I keep walking. I worked too hard and suffered too much to get my boy where he is, and I be damned if some snooty white teacher gonna stop him. As we got closer to the school, Simon ran up ahead of me. I'm sure he went to warn the teacher that his momma was coming and she was mad as hell; she best heed that warning too. When I got inside, I looked around and saw all the little colored children standing next to their rickety desks. Then I spot a young white woman standing in the corner, smiling. "Humph, What she smiling 'bout?" This white teacher don't know who she messing with.

Simon stepped up and said, "Momma, please meet my new teacher Miss Blair."

I was just 'bout to let her have it, before I realized what he said. "Miss Blair?" I asked.

The young woman stepped out the shadows; I squint my eyes to get a better look at her. She had a sweet face, one I sort of knew. Again, I said "Miss Blair?"

"Yes, Beulah, it's me, Sara, Sara Blair from Natchez. You helped raised me, remember?" Without saying another word we ran to each other and hugged; I couldn't believe it. What a miracle this is! My former slave owner child teaching right long side my former slave child. Ain't God good?

Me and Miss Sara met up later and spent hours talking about the past. She told me her mother grew even more bitter after I left, because all her slaves started leaving. Said she still carries a lot of anger toward me and believes I was ungrateful for all she had done for me and colored people. I was reminded of the awful screaming match I had with her mother the day I left so long ago. I understand now that there was nothing I could have said or done that would have changed her mother's mind about me or all colored people. Miss Blair may hate me, but I don't hate her; I don't hate no white people. Hate is a hard thing to carry, and my life is far too blessed to waste time on hate. Young Miss Sara said the older she got, the more she realized just how wrong slavery was; she tried to convince her mother, but she was too old and set in her ways, so she just gave up on her. She told me about a brief period after the war ended called "Reconstruction, where whites created laws that looked out for former slaves and even elected some colored men to Congress, right there in Mississippi. That sure was hard for me to believe, but I don't think she would lie to me. It ain't last long before, angry whites began overturning those new laws and threw all the colored politicians outta office.

THE FIRST COLORED SENATOR AND REPRESENTATIVES,
In the 41ˢᵗ and 42ⁿᵈ Congress of the United States

Life for free colored folk in Mississippi returned to the way it was before slavery ended; if anything, it got even worse. That's when she said she realized the South would never change that whites would never be fair or willing to share power with colored folks. Growing up in Mississippi, Miss Sara saw the hatefulness that destroyed so many lives, but she wasn't blinded by the false beliefs so many other whites hide behind and allowed slavery to persist for so long.

She told me she could no longer live in such an unfair and oppressive system, where whites continually blocked change and mistreated colored people at every turn. That's why she moved north, ending up in Ohio. Miss Sara is a good woman; even as a young child, I could see the good in her.

Goes to show, children of slave owners don't always grow up to be slave owners too and dat not all white people are bad, no more than all colored people are good. There's good and bad in both, cuz we all human.

Miss Sara let me and other older, colored folks sit in her classroom and learn right along with the children. She often spent time teaching me in the evenings and on weekends too. I learned a lot, but what Miss Sara taught me most is something she probably never expected to and that was "It don't matter the color of your skin or your stage of life. What matters most is what's in your heart." Her dedication proves that those who came long before us contributed to or suffered from slavery, but we can all rise above our past and learn to have compassion and love for each other. Miss Sara dedicated her life to making sure colored children get educated. Her and Miss Kincaid became "Life Partners" and are now doing missionary work in Africa. I still receive postcards from them every now and then.

Life Changer

My life has changed so much since leaving Mississippi fifteen years ago, that when I think back on it, I can hardly believe what I been through. I'm in my fifties now, and my life has settled down quite a bit. I made a decent life for myself here in Ohio. The little laundry business I started when I first arrived has grown and remains the only one in town. I did so well I was able to hire other colored women to work in the business with me so they can take care of themselves and their families the same way I did. I also met a fine colored gentleman name Oscar; Rev. Oscar Robinson to be exact. After escaping from a cruel master in Kentucky, he lived as a free man for many years, right here in Ohio. He spent many years trying to find his wife and their five children, who were sold off. He never found his wife or three of his children and never learned what happened to them, but eventually, he found his two youngest children Gracie and Luke. They were enslaved together in Missouri, where he purchased their freedom and brought them back to Ohio. He was very active in the Underground Railroad and helped hundreds of slaves escape into Canada, but he remained in Ohio with his now-grown children.

Rev. Robinson; I always call him by his rightful title out of respect; the respect he was denied for so many years. He's an amazing God-fearing man; we have a lot in common and enjoy each other's company. After years of being alone, the idea of having someone in my life is something I never dreamed I would ever have. We married eight years ago and moved to Chillicothe, Ohio, where we started an African Methodist Episcopal church where he still pastors. My son Simon is twenty-five years old now; he grew up to be a fine young man.

He kept up his education and now teaches at Oberlin College the first college in the United States to admit colored students. Simon and Gracie, Rev. Robinson's daughter, married each other and have blessed us with three of the loveliest grandchildren God ever blew breath in Abigail, Simon Jr., and baby Abe. The church has a large congregation made up of both colored and white members as well as several mixed-race people. Many of 'em were the sons and daughters of wealthy, white Southern fathers and former slave mothers. They moved north and settled here in Ohio with the aid of their white fathers, who were unwilling to acknowledge their mixed-race children due to the social capital they would lose, but were willing to pay for their education as long as they moved on and stayed away.

It was a lovely Sunday morning and the church was full; my whole family was present. Gracie was singing in the choir, and Simon was playing the piano. Gracie has the voice of an angel. I always enjoy her singing. I was singing along with my eyes closed as I rocked baby Abe to sleep. I listened as Rev. Robinson extended the "Hand of Fellowship" like he does every Sunday. I had barely opened my eyes, when I saw a handsome, young colored fellow approach the altar. I watched as he came forward; his gait looked somewhat familiar to me. Rev. Robinson reached out to shake his hand to welcome the strange man to our church When all of a sudden, Simon hit a wrong key and let out a huge gasp. The whole church came to a hush; nobody moved. I slowly stood up and handed the baby to my granddaughter who was sitting next to me. I moved toward the altar to get a better look at this young man, and when he turned around, I just about fainted. It was Abraham, my son who went off so many years ago aboard the ship that brought us here to Ohio. He wrapped his arms around me and we held each other tight for a long time.

I kept whispering "You did come back. You did come back. I always knew you would. Thank you, Jesus!" The family and all the church members gathered around; everyone was crying and praising God. I couldn't help but wish my Noni was here with us, but I could feel her presence. Rev. Robinson was so inspired he went on to give a stirring sermon that had the whole church up on their feet the whole time. He ended his moving message with "Thank you, God, for delivering us from evil, for thine is the kingdom the power, and the glory forever and ever. Let the church say, *Amen*." What a joyous time! Praise God! I picked up baby Abe and handed him over to his namesake, Uncle Abraham. Life don't come with no promises; you just have to make the best of it, and I did my best!

The End

CHAPTER 4
Philadelphia, Pennsylvania, 1964

MY LIFE AS A COLORED GIRL

Geraldine is my name, but it's corny and I don't like it, so call me Gerri. I'm a young colored girl from West Philly. Growing up in the 1960s had both advantages and disadvantages. The world was rapidly changing, practically before my eyes, but I had no idea just how much it would change. I lived with both my parents and a younger brother in a stable, middle-class community. Many of my friends came from two-parent households as well. Most of the adults in my neighborhood had good jobs as government, city, factory and blue-collar workers. And there were a good number of housewives who kept an eye on all the neighborhood kids, whether you belonged to them or not. If they caught you doing something wrong, they would get on you then your parents would finish the job when they got home no questions asked. Even though my parents just had secondary school educations they both had good paying jobs. My dad was a supervisor with the city transit system, and my mom an assembly worker for a major electronics company. She was awarded for her work on Explorer One; the first successfully launched U.S. satellite. They provided me and my little brother a good life; we never wanted for anything. I attended public schools, where most of my teachers were Jewish women; they were patient and most seemed committed to teaching colored children, but we weren't always as attentive or as well behaved as maybe we should have been.

I was more social than I was academic, but I managed to get by. I was a lively teen with a great personality and made friends easily. One of my friends was Janice Kaplan, a white girl. In fact, she was the only white girl in our predominantly colored high school. There were a few white boys too, but she was the only white girl at the time. Jan had a great personality and everyone liked her. She had a naturally dark complexion and in the summer would get as dark as a light-skinned colored girl. Her hair was dark brown, frizzy, and it looked like Negro hair which made her fit in even more, but you could still tell she was a white girl, or maybe mixed. People often asked her what she was, which always ticked her off; sometimes she would tell them she was South African and that would shut them up. Ha! Jan and I hung out a lot together, mostly in school. We liked many of the same things and belonged to many of the same school clubs and groups. Both of us lived in walking distance of our school exactly ten blocks away, but in totally opposite directions. She lived on Forty-second and Spruce Sts. and I lived on Fifty-second and Spruce Sts.

Jan's neighborhood was called Spruce Hill; and located near the University of Pennsylvania, where her dad was a college professor and her mother an elementary school teacher. University of Pennsylvania Hospital is in the same area. Most of the people who lived in her community were students, teachers, doctors, and most of them were white. The streets were hilly, clean, and lined with big, beautiful spruce trees; hence the name Spruce Hill. My neighborhood is just called West Philly, sometimes South Side. I remember when we had spruce streets too, but the city sprayed them with pesticides. The trees eventually died; then they cut them all down. I sure wish they hadn't done that. The streets weren't as clean as those in Spruce Hill, because people around my way often threw their random trash right on the street; I knew better than to litter.

Jan and I often walked each other home after school. I would walk her all the way home, but when she walked me home, she never crossed Fiftieth St. She said her parents told her not to go any further, because it wasn't safe. There was gang activity going on around my way. Gangs with names like the Moon, Creek and Hoops to name a few, were fighting each other over turf. My parents said they were bringing the neighborhood down. It probably wasn't safe for me either, but I never had any problems.

We Were Friends

Jan and I had a lot of fun together, sometimes getting into mischief. One time we went in a grocery store near our school; the manager was so busy keeping an eye on me to make sure I didn't steal anything that Jan was able to stuff her book bag full of loose candy: Mary Jane's, Good & Plenty's, Squirrel Nuts, and Bazooka bubble gums, then we ran out the store laughing; it was so funny. I only met Jan's parents once, when her mother spotted us outside her house talking and invited me in. Both her mom and dad were hippie-type-looking people. They began telling me how important it was to have their only child grow up in a diverse community with Negroes and other ethnic groups. They went on and on, until I finally said I had to get home. It seemed like they were trying to prove something to me, but I couldn't figure out what it was. It didn't matter to me that Jan was white. I liked her anyway; we were friends.

We both were fascinated with Bandstand, a popular teen dance show that was nationally televised in Philly. We watched it every day after school as we talked on the phone about who was the cutest couple or who danced the best. Interestingly, the show was filmed just blocks away from our school at Forty-sixth and Market Sts. The show was moving to California, and we heard they were only going to be taping a few more shows in Philly. We couldn't understand why Dick Clark, the host, would do that, considering the show was so popular. Anyway, they were looking for dancers, so we decided to go try out after school the next day.

We walked the few blocks to the TV station, WPVI, where the show was being taped. But when we got there, there was a line wrapped clear around the corner full of white kids. Many of them had arrived there by El, the elevated train that ran down Market St, and stopped right in front of the studio. They came from different parts of the city: South Philly, North East, Kensington, and other mostly white neighborhoods. There were very few colored kids in line; even when you watched the program, you could only spot a colored kid every now and then. I was a much better dancer than Jan; we practiced dancing together all the time, we did the cha-cha, shotgun, and the twist; a popular dance started in Philly by a colored guy named Chubby Checker. Jan didn't have much rhythm, but if you held her hand, she was able to follow.

We stood in line for hours before we made it to the studio door; I happened to be standing in front of Jan. I smiled at the young white man who was deciding who to let in, hoping he would choose me, but he looked right past me as if I was invisible. He pointed to Jan and told her to come in; she hesitated at first, but when the guy asked her if she was coming in or not, she quickly stepped through the door. She looked back at me for a second before going inside. Even though she made it in, she only got to sit on the sidelines, which I would have been happy to do too, if I had the opportunity. I didn't hold it against her though.

A few weeks later, we signed up for the school talent show. We planned to sing "Please Mr. Postman" by the Marvelettes, with two other girls. I was the lead singer, and put the group together. I didn't ask Jan to be in the group at first because she was tone deaf and couldn't carry a note in a bucket and she knew it, but she bugged me so much I finally let her in the group. We practiced singing for weeks before the show; I choreographed some great moves and we had cute, matching outfits. Despite Jan's sour notes, we somehow managed to win anyway. Some said the only reason we did was because we were the only group with a white girl in it, I didn't care what anyone said. I knew it was because we performed better.

Country Woman

The next evening, my parents left my little brother with a sitter and took me with them to a meeting. They belonged to a community activist group called "Citizens for Progress," which focused on voter's registration for the upcoming 1964 presidential election. They needed me to stuff and write out envelopes. I listened as my mom and her friends kept going on about some woman they had invited to

Philadelphia to speak to the group. They were real excited about the powerful speaker and how much she was going to fire up their group. They had purchased the woman a bus ticket to travel to Philly from Mississippi. They mentioned her name, but I had never heard of her before or ever read about her in the *JET* magazine. My parents had a monthly subscription, and I read it cover to cover every month, so she couldn't be that much of a big deal, or so I thought. It was getting late; it was a school night and I was tired. My mom saw me yawning and told me to go upstairs and lie down; she promised they would be ready to leave as soon as the speaker woman arrived. I didn't want to lie down in someone else's bed. I'd much rather go home and get in my own bed but I was really getting tired, so I went on.

My dad was headed out to pick the woman up from the bus station; I stopped and gave him a quick hug. I'm not sure how long I was asleep, but it couldn't have been too long when I heard a lot of noise coming from downstairs, so I got up to go see what was going on. The woman they had been talking about for hours had finally arrived. I sat on the top step and peeked through the banisters. I wanted to see who this woman they were making such a big deal about was. Who I saw was a short, heavy-set colored woman with large breasts; the buttons on it looked like they might pop off at any minute. She had a heavy Southern drawl, and she was so loud I was sure neighbors several doors away could hear her. She was talking about going to Atlantic City the next day. I looked on for a while as everybody held onto her every word, but I wasn't very impressed with her, so I went to lie back down.

A short time later, I was awakened again by the same little colored woman I had seen earlier. She was pushing me aside and telling me to move over to make room for her in the bed so she could lie down, but I immediately got up and let her have the whole bed to herself. The next night, I was watching TV with my parents, the evening news was on. There she was, the same Country woman I had seen the night before, right there on the TV screen in black and white. I knew it was her because she had on the same dress she had on the night before. I was amazed; she was in Atlantic City, just like she said she would be. She was at the 1964 Democratic Convention and was trying to push through a group of white men who refused to let her sit with the all-white Mississippi delegation. She represented the Mississippi

Freedom Democratic Party, which included Negroes, and they didn't recognize that organization. Later, she was shown giving a passionate speech to the Mississippi Credentials Committee about the violence and discrimination she and many other colored people faced in the South while trying to register to vote.

I was absolutely riveted by her composure and ability to deliver a stirring message in such a plain-spoken manner. She was absolutely amazing! She became known for her infamous quote: "All my life I've been sick and tired. Now I'm sick and tired of being sick and tired."

Her name is Mrs. Fannie Lou Hamer, and she made an impression on me that would last a lifetime. Because of her, I learned you don't have to be highly educated; you just need to be courageous enough to stand for something. My parents already exposed me to the importance of voting. I didn't know it then, but Mrs. Hamer sparked a light in me that made me realize what it meant to be a social activist. I knew I had to do all I could to help my people; colored people to ensure we have the right to vote, move forward, and be treated fairly.

How I Helped Kill the President

My mom woke me up for school; like she does every morning. She started telling me the same thing she does every day before she leaves. "Open the blinds before you leave, clean the kitchen, and take something out the freezer for dinner, and don't forget to pick your brother up after school."

"Okay, okay, every morning you say the same thing. Geez!"

"Hey!" she yelled up the steps to me. "You better watch your mouth, young lady. Don't make me come up there."

I rolled my eyes, knowing darn well she couldn't see me. I started to ask her if I could stay home from school today but I knew she would never go for that. She even made me go to school when I was sick, and I was really sick a few of those times.

My mom left with my brother to drop him off at a new government-subsidized program for inner-city preschoolers called Head Start before she went on to work. After she left, I decided I was going to play hooky from school; it was a spur-of-the-moment decision, but one I felt I had to make it.

I was focused on a big school play that was coming up in a few weeks. I had auditioned for the lead role and was one of four finalists Jan was one of them. I wasn't at all worried because none of the others could touch me, and for sure, Jan was no real threat. My drama coach, Miss Marilyn Coleman, was a sharp; colored woman. She wore brightly colored Bohemian clothes, big earrings, and had a shaved head. She looked really cool but somewhat unusual for a colored woman; in Philly anyway. Not only was she our drama coach, she was an English teacher. She also was a professional actress and appeared in several local film productions and stage plays in New York City. She told me she eventually planned to move to Los Angeles to pursue work in films. The play included a lot of singing, dancing, and acting, and I was good at all three, so I knew I was a definite shoe-in. I was really excited about the play. Jan was excited too, but not nearly as much as I was. Just last week, Miss Coleman took me aside and told me how impressed she was that I had not only memorized my lines, but all the other cast members lines too and how helpful that would be if I ever decided to become a professional actress. What? That's exactly what I planned to do. Coming from Miss Coleman, that meant a lot to me; she really blew my mind and I wanted to impress her. Maybe when she becomes a star, she'll fly me out to LA to be her understudy; how cool would that be? My head was swimming with dreams of stardom.

A rehearsal was scheduled after school today. I had spent the previous evening on the phone helping Jan memorize her lines and how to deliver them with proper emphasis before my mom told me to hang up and go to bed. I had been on the phone so long that the bulb inside the dial of my pink Princess phone had burned a little round mark on the side of my face; I sure hope it clears up before the play.

I needed to study my script so I could be fully prepared for rehearsal that evening. This was a role of a lifetime, and since I'm going to be the principal player, I have to be perfect. I didn't tell Jan I wouldn't be in school today, because I hadn't planned to hooky. I know she's probably going to wonder where I was, but I'll explain when I see her later this evening at rehearsal. Once I decided to stay home from school, I pulled my covers back over my head and went back to sleep. *What the heck!* I figured. I may as well get some extra shut-eye. I woke up a little later feeling refreshed and ready to go.

I showered and got dressed in the same clothes I had laid out the night before to wear to school that day. I ate a bowl of Rice Krispies; I liked the "Snap, Crackle, and Pop sounds." I stirred up a glass of orange Tang to sip on while I rehearsed my lines. I was still practicing later that afternoon and had the TV on but had the volume turned down so it wouldn't interfere with me practicing my lines out loud, but so I could still watch my favorite soap opera *As the World Turns*. I noticed the program had been interrupted and the words *NEWS FLASH* scrolled across the bottom of the TV screen. Walter Kronkite appeared; I knew it was him because my dad watches his newscast every evening after dinner. At first I got nervous, because I thought I had lost track of time and it was later than I thought it was. If that was the case, my mom and dad were due home from work soon. I still hadn't picked up my brother, made my bed, or washed the dishes nothing I'm supposed to do when I get home from school. But when I looked at the clock, it was just 1:10. *Phew*, I thought as I swept imaginary sweat from my brow.

I still couldn't hear what Walter Kronkite was saying, so I went over to the TV and turned the volume up. He looked nervous there was a lit cigarette sitting in an ashtray next to him. He must've been smoking before he came on the air; I never noticed that in any of his previous broadcasts. I continued to read my lines out loud. A few minutes later, I heard or thought I heard Mr. Kronkite say *"The president has been shot!"* Huh, what was that? What did he say? The president, President who? President of what?

Then he repeated what he said, but added more "President Kennedy has been shot in Dallas, Texas." Now he had my full attention. "President Kennedy was shot?" I repeated. I couldn't wrap my brain around that; I must not have heard him correctly. President John F. Kennedy was my parent's favorite president. They even had his picture hanging on the wall right next to a white Jesus holding his purple heart outside of his chest, which really bugs me, but that's another story. Wow! I sure hope the president will be okay. I turned the TV back down and went back to studying my lines and thinking back to what Miss Coleman had said to me about becoming an actress. I have this role in the bag, because no one else in my drama class was as good as I was at least not as far as I was concerned. The TV got my attention again.

Walter Kronkite was back on the TV screen, so I went over and turned the volume back up, just as I did, I heard him say *"Three shots were fired at President Kennedy's motorcade in downtown Dallas. The President was raced to Parkland Memorial Hospital. A half hour later, he was pronounced dead."*

President Kennedy is dead? Oh my God! How sad! What's going to happen to Jackie, his pretty wife, and their children Caroline and little John-John? They're so cute. I need to talk to someone. I ran to the phone, picked it up, and started dialing Jan's phone number, but then I realized she was probably still in school. I was so confused and for some reason scared too. I didn't know what to do. I ran to the window, where I still had the venetian blinds closed; I usually open them before I leave for school, as my Mom reminds me to do every morning, but I left them closed today because I couldn't take a chance that nosy Miss Stewart the neighbor who lives directly across the street, would be able to see I was home when I should have been in school. I slowly raised one of the slats and looked out. As I was peeking through the blinds, I saw Miss Stewart come out of her house. She was holding her head and crying. Then Miss Cookie, her next-door neighbor, came out, then Miss Mary on the other side of her came out, and they all were crying and shaking their heads. It was unbelievable sight! What's going on? I thought. Is the world coming to an end? Now everyone was coming out of their homes, and they all were standing around talking to each other. I wanted to run out and join them, but I couldn't because I wasn't supposed to be home. I can't believe what's happening! Of all days, why did I choose today to play hooky? Then it hit me, school!

I wondered what's happening in school. Wonder if they let out early? I hope so, because then I can go outside and be with everyone else. The phone rang, I ran to answer it, but just before I picked it up, I remembered I couldn't, because I wasn't supposed to be home. This is too much; what am I going to do? The volume on the TV was still up; they were now showing the street where President Kennedy was shot and interviewing people who witnessed the shooting. I watched for a while, but it was making me even more anxious, so I turned the TV back down. I heard the screen door open. Oh shit! It's my mom! I watched as some mail came shooting through the mail slot, it was just the mailman dropping off the mail. My heart was beating out of my chest and my armpits were sweating. I felt like I was going to pass out, so I sat down, took a swig of my Tang and tried to get myself together. Too much was happening all at the same time. I looked at the clock again; it was 2:15. I usually get home from school around 3:30; unless I pick my brother up first then I get home a little later. This is the longest day of my life. I feel like I'm in prison or something. None of this would have happened if I hadn't played hooky from school today. The president wouldn't have been shot and I wouldn't be in this mess I feel so guilty. Finally, 3:30 rolled around now I can leave the house.

I went around opening all the blinds, made up my bed, cleaned the kitchen, and took some ground beef out the freezer to thaw out for my mom to cook for dinner when she got home later. I made sure all my chores were done. Then I got ready to leave to go pick up my little brother. Before I left, I decided to grab my book bag so I could look normal not that anything that about today was at all normal. I unlocked the door and stepped out.

Miss Stewart was still on her porch, I could feel her staring at my back; it was stinging. Then I heard her say "Gerri, are you coming or going?"

I turned around and acted surprised. With my key still in the lock, I said "Huh, who me? I'm coming."

"Coming from where?" she asked.

"Ssschool, I'm coming from school" I stuttered.

She kept on, "Oh really, well I didn't see you come up the street, and the blinds were closed all day and now they're open."

Geez, why doesn't she mind her damn business? I thought to myself. I pretended not to hear her and hurried off. All the streets were buzzing about President Kennedy; everyone was talking about it. All the newspaper headlines had the same thing "President Kennedy is Dead!" I don't want to be reminded of what I've been through today. Later that afternoon, Miss Coleman called to tell me tonight's rehearsal was cancelled because of the president's assassination. I was so disappointed; I went through all that for nothing.

The next day at school, Jan came up to me.

"Where were you yesterday?"

"*Girlll*, you have no idea what I've been through."

"Did you hear about President Kennedy?"

"Yeah, of course I did. Well, I was there through the whole thing."

"You were in Dallas, Texas?"

"Nooo, stupid! I was home, but I saw the whole thing on TV."

"Why were you home anyway? Were you sick?"

"No, I was fine. I decided to stay home so I could finish studying my lines for the play, but rehearsal was canceled, so it didn't even matter. Anyway, Miss Coleman still plans to make her announcement after rehearsal, so let's go," and we both ran off.

Rehearsal went well, and as usual, I nailed my lines. Before Miss Coleman made her announcement, she had us all bow our heads for a moment of silent prayer for President Kennedy. I said a short prayer but kept looking out one eye to see if anyone else was done, because I didn't want to be the first. Miss Coleman was really taking her time making her announcement she kept going on and on about how difficult her decision was and how all the auditions were so good, blah, blah, blah. I tuned her out and started reviewing in my head how I would dramatically act when she called my name. I heard her say something and dramatically swooned to the floor lightly as if had fainted, careful not to let my head hit the floor. I lay there a few minutes waiting for Jan or one of the other kids to come pick me up, but no one did, so I just got up on my own. I was brushing off my clothes when I noticed everyone clapping, but they weren't clapping for me. Miss Coleman hadn't called my name at all. Instead, she announced that Jan had won the title role. Jan? Jan? Are you kidding me? She can't even act! Everyone was congratulating her; I couldn't believe it. I can act rings around that girl! Most of the time, she can't even remember her lines, and Miss Coleman constantly has to keep telling her to speak up.

I was so angry! Jan couldn't even look at me; she knew she didn't deserve that role. I had spent hours teaching her how to say her lines and how to act them out, and she never even thanked me. What was Miss Coleman thinking? I looked over at her she saw the look of disappointment on my face and came over and gave me a hug, but I kept my arms folded in front of me.

As she hugged me, she whispered in my ear "I'm so sorry. Please forgive me. You'll understand later."

Huh, what did she mean by that? Even though she had given me another role, it had fewer lines and I wouldn't have as much stage time as I wanted, but I was still determined to make my role unforgettable. I kept studying my lines and practicing the different tones of voice I needed to use to say *"Stop! Where do you think you're going?"*

Then, I was to run up to Jan and spin her around. I practiced with my old Chatty Cathy doll, but every time I spun the doll around, it fell down and I had to keep standing it back up. I guess I was taking my anger out on Chatty Cathy.

The play was just okay, but I was superb even strangers and my family and friends said I was the best. Jan bombed just like I knew she would. Serves Miss Coleman right; she was jive for not choosing me in the first place. But when I looked at her, she had a sad look on her face; I noticed a tear in her eye. She resigned shortly after that.

Years passed, and just like she had predicted, Miss Coleman was featured in a Richard Pryor movie and several other major films and numerous theatre productions; seeing her on the big screen was so boss! As I watched her, I thought about what she had whispered to me a while back. Knowing what I do now, I can only assume that she was probably pressured to choose Jan over me or any other colored girl to star in the play. That was so unfair! Little did I know how much more unfairness I would face in years to come.

It's a Light-skinned Thing

Jan and I continued to hang out together and by our senior year we had become really close. We talked all the time, mostly about boys. She never mentioned any boy in particular that she liked plenty of colored boys liked her though, but she never dated any of them that I know of and I would have if she did. Jan and I were passing a group of ball players after school one day; whenever girls pass by, the boys always start catcalling them. I heard one of them shout "Hey, Foxy Brown," and when I turned to look, I saw one of the boys, pointing at me. I swear I heard music and everything began to move in slow motion.

The boy's name was Johnny Duke; we started talking and I waved Jan to go on. Johnny was on the basketball team. "Go, Speed Boys!"

He spent more time on the bench than he did in the game, because he was always hurt, but I liked him anyway; he was so smooth. He was really cute; he was tall, bow-legged, and had a thick neck, arms, and calves, just like a jock. He was also light-skinned with curly hair; I'm brown-skinned but I was more attracted to light-skinned boys; like they say; opposites attract. Jan often teased me about Johnny; she even made up a jingle based on the song Duke of Earl.

She sang *"Duke, Duke, Duke, Duke of Curls."*

"Cut it out!" I said laughing. Johnny and I planned to go to the prom together. Back in those days, parents met before the prom to discuss how their kids were going to get to and from the prom and what they were going to do after. My parents had met Johnny before and they were cool with him. But when I went with my mom to Johnny's house to meet his mom, you could tell she was not pleased he had chosen me for his prom date. She was a high-yellow woman, as my mom called her. She was cordial but standoffish, she never offered us a seat or anything to drink, so we kept our meeting short.

The next day, I was telling Jan about my awkward visit with Johnny's mom. She started telling me about all the colored guys who had asked her to the prom, including Johnny; but had turned them all down because she wasn't going to the prom. Her parents had planned a family trip the same time as the prom, so she would be away. I found that interesting for two reasons; first of all, why would they do that, knowing their daughter would miss her senior prom? Could it be they thought it was okay for her to hang out with Negroes, just don't date one, *hmmm*. Secondly, I couldn't believe she hadn't told me Johnny had asked her to the prom, and when I asked her why, she said she didn't want to hurt my feelings. Hurt my feelings? I told her that not telling me hurt my feelings even more. I thought we were friends and shared everything with each other; I began to wonder what else she hadn't told me.

The prom was a week away, and I wasn't sure if Johnny was still going to take me, because I hadn't seen or heard from him since meeting his mom. He later called to tell me he broke his leg and couldn't go to the prom, but when I asked his teammates if they knew about him breaking his leg, no one knew anything about it. I knew it was just an excuse and the real reason was because his mom wouldn't allow him to take me to the prom; I was devastated. My mom came to my rescue, but I wish she hadn't. She arranged for a neighbor boy to take me to the prom. He wasn't exactly my type, not at all. He was short, skinny, and wore big, thick, always-smudged eyeglasses; he looked like *Willie the Worm,* yuck!

I had a miserable time and ducked him all night so no one would know he was my date; I was home before midnight. Johnny didn't attend the prom.

Jan and I remained friends, but we weren't nearly as close as we had been in the past. Jan had tried out for the cheerleading team and made it. I'm not sure how, because she had no rhythm and was kind of bottom-heavy. She wasn't able to jump or kick very high like cheerleaders need to do, but that's their problem. Most of the girls on the cheerleading squad were light-skinned, and I'm sure the only reason they chose her was because she was white but looked like a light-skinned colored girl. Like the saying goes "White is right, yellow is a nice fellow, black stay back." Jan started hanging around her new cheerleader friends and began acting stuck-up like the rest of them. When it was just the two of us together, she was herself; but as soon as one of her cheerleader friends came around, she changed her attitude toward me.

I overheard one of them call me a *Booga-Bear* and I went after her, but Jan and some other girls got between us. I didn't like those girls, because they always acted like they were better than me; I knew they didn't like me either, just because I'm brown-skinned.

There's a common belief in colored communities that light-skinned Negroes are better than the dark-skinned ones. It's a holdover from slavery; white slave owners often raped slave women and their children had lighter skin. Supposedly, whites treated them better than they did the darker ones even though we were all slaves, don't forget. It's just one more thing white people used to draw a wedge between colored people, and it apparently worked, because here we are generations later, continuing to perpetuate the same belief. It's stupid and we should stop it!

Big Mistake!

It was time for graduation and I was glad to finally be done with high school. I looked forward to hanging out with my friends over the summer and leaving for college in the fall. Most of all, I looked forward to being on my own, making my own decisions, and doing what I wanted to do, when I wanted to do it. That summer was the best one I ever had. Jan spent that summer in the Hamptons with her parents, so we didn't get to see each other much, and I was cool with that. After hanging out with Jan all those years, I began to realize just how different my life as a colored girl was in a world that didn't place as much value on me as it did a white girl. Jan never made me feel different, but the fact of the matter is we are. I'm not even sure she recognized the privileges that automatically came with her white skin, but I'm sure she'll find out soon enough. I don't blame her; that's just the way it is.

I began hanging out with my other girlfriends; colored ones. We went to Willow Grove Amusement Park, had a ball at Smith's playground in North Philly, went swimming at Kelly's Pool, and hung out at Fairmount Park during the Greek Picnic a favorite summer affair for Negro fraternities, and did lots of other fun things. I had a great time! Also, for the first time, my parents let me go to Atlantic City with my friends for the weekend. This was a really big deal! It was the same weekend another popular Negro fraternity affair was going on called; "Omega By the Sea." I think my parents figured since I was leaving for college in a few weeks, I was mature enough and trusted me to behave myself. *Big mistake!* I was never a drinker or a smoker, and I certainly didn't do drugs, but I loved to dance and just have fun; I partied my ass off. My parents didn't know it, but Johnny was going to be there and we had planned to hang out together. That weekend, I lost my virginity.

Jan and I stayed in touch for a short while after graduation; her father got a position at University of California Berkeley, and they moved to California. She sent me a few postcards and we talked on the phone a couple of times about me visiting her in California, but it never happened; eventually, we lost contact. It was 1965 and I was attending Shaw University in Raleigh, North Carolina. It was at the height of the Civil Rights Movement; the summer before was called Freedom Summer.

Like the rest of the nation, we watched on television how whites were treating young colored people in the South brutally beating and turning hoses and dogs on them it was really scary. My parents were nervous about me attending school in the South, with all that was going on down there. They made me promise to stay on campus and not to get involved in all that civil rights stuff as they called it. Other than sleepover camp, which I attended for a few weeks during summer when I was younger, this would be my first time away from home and on my own for a long period of time.

I was never afraid to speak up for myself or for others for that matter. I guess you could say I was kind of a rabble-rouser, but I prefer to be called a "maverick." My mom, on the other hand, called me a "big mouth."

She said to me "Gerri, one of these days, your mouth is going to write a check that your ass can't cash." Her words would later come back to haunt me.

Before I boarded the train at 30th Street Station, my dad said to me "Listen, the way we handle things up North is very different than how they do in the South. White people down there are crazy; I want you to be careful. I'm sending you to school to get an education. Do your school work, mind your business, watch your mouth, and stay out of trouble, you hear me?"

"Yes, Daddy, I will."

We hugged and I was on my way.

The Civil Rights Movement Is No Joke!

After just a few months on campus, I got caught up in all the civil rights activities that were happening both on and off campus. I wanted to be a part of the movement and began signing up for meetings and participated in demonstrations and boycotts that were going on in the nearby town of Raleigh. I attended a meeting where a fiery, young college student from Howard University; Stokely Carmichael was speaking. I had seen Dr. King on television many times making speeches about nonviolence, but Stokely took an opposite position. He was far more radical and believed colored people should take a more activist role even use civil disobedience when and where needed. He called it "Black Power" and said we should stop calling ourselves colored or Negroes like my parents and others their age call themselves. From that point on, I never referred to myself as colored or Negro ever again, I was black! I stopped pressing my hair too, so it could grow out naturally and I could wear an afro. Ironically, my first major civil disobedience activity happened, in all places, New York City. The Student Non-Violent Coordinating Committee better known as SNCC, had arranged for a bus to pick up a group of us from campus and take us to New York City to participate in a march or a walk-in at the United Nations; I wasn't sure what it was. Why the United Nations? To this day, I have no idea. I also had no idea what I had signed up for or what to expect, but when the day came and my name was called, I just went along; call it peer pressure. The bus trip to New York was actually fun; along the way, we sang freedom songs and listened as students from other colleges pumped us up with radical speeches.

A young white woman was flitting around ordering others around, and they were all listening to her. She was stocky-built, had bright red hair and a strong personality. I first noticed her at the meeting where I heard Stokely Carmichael speak. She was on stage with him, running around doing things like she was in charge. I found out later that she was a graduate student from Western College for Women in Oxford, Ohio. I was sitting in the front of the bus when she asked me to hand her some boxes that were under the seat I was in. I reached down and handed them to her; she thanked me and asked me my name. I told her and she introduced herself.

"I'm Priscilla, but everyone calls me Prissy." We shook hands.

"Hello, Prissy, nice to meet you."

Prissy sat next to me; she told me she was a member of SNCC and was a trained "Freedom Rider."

I had no idea there was such training; she went on to tell me how she volunteered to come South to teach colored people how to register to vote. She said she was supposed to be in Philadelphia, Mississippi, at the same time three civil rights workers: Chaney, Goodman, and Schwerner were killed.

"Weren't you scared?" I asked her.

"Yes, but I'm outraged by all the injustices going on in the South. Black people are citizens too and have a right to vote. Every day, more volunteers are joining us; they can't stop us all. Just like the song says 'We Shall Not Be Moved.'"

I was impressed with her bravery and conviction. It reminded of how Mrs. Hamer stood up and was beaten and threatened; she didn't stop either. Now, I was in this to win this! I began helping Prissy hand out fried chicken sandwiches that some church ladies had prepared for us to eat along the way because we couldn't stop at segregated places in the South; they also had lots of water coolers on the bus. My parents had no idea I would be in New York, when I clearly should have been at school, and I prayed to God they would never find out.

When we arrived in New York, there were hundreds of buses filled with loads of students, primarily white ones from schools all over the country: Boston, Chicago, and as far as San Francisco. Seeing all these like-minded, young black and white people carrying signs to show where they all came from all in one place really inspired me.

The planners of the march were smart; they had arranged for thousands of boxed lunches and coffee stations to be placed all around the area; it was a great idea, because we were all tired and hungry from the long bus rides. However, what the planners had not given any thought to apparently was where all these people were going to use the bathroom.

Almost immediately, stores began closing their doors and refusing entry into their business to use the bathrooms. That led to people mostly guys, peeing in doorways and alleys. We didn't come all this way for nothing, and the march or protest, whatever it was, still had to go on. They instructed us to lock arms and walk sidebyside, row after row, along the flag-lined corridor toward the United Nations.

Somehow, I ended up in the front row locked arm in arm with Prissy on one side and a white boy who I had never met or even seen before on the other. But we were all on the same mission; hundreds of people on both sides of me and hundreds more behind me, as far as I could see. I could only imagine how formidable we must have looked, and here I was, little old me, a black girl from West Philly, marching down this amazing street that represents all the countries of the world. Who knew? I was walking and singing protest songs "We Shall Overcome" and "Ain't Gonna Let Nobody Turn Me Around"; I sang the songs loud and proud. I was walking or should I say being pulled along in lock step with others. I looked up ahead and saw a phalanx of boot cops on horses stretched across the street in front of us; but we remained locked arm in arm, marching forward and singing.

Prissy kept shouting, "What do we want?"

And the crowd responded "Freedom!"

"When do we want it?"

"Now!"

She kept saying it, over and over again. We were quickly approaching the cops, they didn't appear to be moving back. The closer we got, the larger their horses looked to me. We got right up to them; we were so close I could feel the horses' breath mixing with mine, and it wasn't pleasant. All of a sudden, the cops started moving their horses, but not backward they were moving forward right toward us.

So what do we do now? I asked myself. My arms were still locked together with Prissy and the white boy on the other side of me, and they were tightening their grip. Now I'm thinking to myself; how am I going to get out of this? Here I am in New York City about to get trampled by a bunch of horses. How will I ever explain this to my parents? I just hope I die so I never have to.

Out of nowhere, the horses started galloping toward us; they broke through the lines; I was thrown up against the curb.

My shoulder hit a sewer grate and I felt the worse pain I ever did before. I couldn't move; I just lay there in the gutter, paralyzed in pain and fear. All I could see were people's feet and horses' hooves coming toward me, so I covered my head and braced myself to be trampled to death.

Prissy was shaking me "Gerri, get up. We have to get out of here!"

I tried to move, but the pain in my shoulder was excruciating. Prissy pulled me up; I screamed out in pain, and we started running together. *Oh my God!* What am I going to do? I kept thinking. My shoulder was killing me and I was crying. Prissy waved down an ambulance worker; a lot of people were hurt and they were going around seeing who needed help. I was picked up on a stretcher and put in an ambulance. The next thing I remember was waking up in the hospital. Prissy was there.

She said "Gerri, you're gonna be okay. You broke your collarbone."

"My collarbone?" I tried to sit up, but it hurt too much.

"Be still; I found your phone number in your wallet and called your parents."

"What? You did what? What the hell did you do that for?"

"Look, your parents are on their way, but I let them know you were all right, so just rest. They'll be here soon."

"Are you kidding me? What the fuck! Why'd you do that? They're going to kill me! Do you understand that? My parents are going to kill me!"

I started crying uncontrollably and began praying. "God, this is Gerri I hope you can hear me. Please take my life, Lord. Let me die now. I don't care if you send me to heaven or hell, just let me die. Lord, I beg you, please just let me die."

When my parents got there, they didn't say much; they were more concerned if I was all right, but I knew it was just a matter of time before they were going to "tear me a new one." They said very little to me on the ride back home to Philly, and the silence was deafening. I was sitting in the back seat with my annoying little brother who kept asking me, "What's wrong with your arm, Gerri? What happened to your arm?" But I just ignored him. I had on a huge cast that went from my shoulder down to my wrist, with a bar sticking out of my armpit that prevented me from putting my arm down. It hurt like hell, but it made me feel even worse because I looked like an idiot with this monstrosity on. All the way home, my brother kept yelling, "Put your arm down. Put your arm down. Mommy, Gerri keeps putting her arm in my face."

Geez, what a pube! I said to myself. A few days later, I was resting comfortably in my bed and reading *Ebony* magazine, when my parents came in my room, closed the door, and began to hand down the wrath of God on me. One by one, they started throwing questions at me.

"What were you thinking? What the hell were you doing in New York? What did we tell you? Do you know you could have been killed?"

Apparently, the questions they were hurling at me must have been rhetorical, because every time I tried to answer them, they told me to shut up! So I just laid there as they let me have it; plus, I had no real, valid reason for what I did nothing that would have satisfied them anyway. They went on and on. After a while, my mom threw up her hands up in exasperation.

"I have to get out of here before this girl makes me hurt her," she said and left the room.

I was a daddy's girl and usually could shed a few crocodile tears to get my way with him, but not this time that didn't work this time. After he was done, he turned to leave, then stopped, and said "Young lady, you're grounded indefinitely, and by the way, do something about your nappy head." That kind of hurt my feelings, because my afro was growing out and I thought it looked cute.

The next day, Prissy called to see how I was doing; I let her know I was feeling better but I would probably miss the rest of the semester because I would be in a cast for at least six weeks. She told me she was heading to Birmingham, Alabama. Two years earlier, four little black girls were killed in a church bombing there, and she was helping to coordinate a march to honor them. Prissy was certainly committed to the movement.

I somehow wished I could join her, but I've been thinking; maybe I need to find another way to support the effort. The Civil Rights Movement is no joke, and all those young people, blacks as well as whites, really put their lives on the line. Maybe, I should stick to licking and stuffing envelopes; it's certainly safer. I never heard from Prissy anymore after that, but if I know her, she's probably still out there kicking ass and taking names. Many years later, I was scanning through a book about the Black Panthers and saw a photo taken at a rally in California and spotted Prissy in the background with her mouth open and her fist raised. I smiled and thought to myself, *That white girl is something else!* She was "one bad, shut yo' mouth!"

Get a Job

After missing an entire semester of college, my parents sat me down and had a long conversation with me about going back to school. The more I thought about it, the more I realized my heart wasn't really into college and probably never was, if I was truly being honest with myself. I didn't want to waste anymore of my parents' hard-earned money; I realized I was still too immature to be on my own and needed to stay close to home under my parents' guidance a little longer.

That being the case, my dad told me that if I wasn't going back to school, then I would have to get a job, because I couldn't continue living under their roof doing nothing. No problem, I thought. I'll just get a job; I was ready to earn my own money.

I went to the unemployment office and signed up for work, but I soon realized that with no work experience and at just seventeen years old, I wasn't really qualified for much of anything. I found a few odd jobs camp counselor, teacher's aide, but they didn't pay much, and they weren't very interesting either. One day as I was scanning the Classified Ads, I noticed an ad for the telephone company: "Operators Wanted." Umm, that sounds interesting. I showed my mom the ad and asked her what she thought about it.

"You could do that; you speak well.

Yes, I do, I thought.

"You're as qualified as anyone else, but to be honest though a lot has changed since I started out under Jim Crow laws, there's still a lot of racism and bigotry we have to deal with. But I don't want that to stop you; go for it. All they can say is no, and you just keep trying."

The ad said they were accepting applications at the corporate offices downtown, so I planned to go and apply the next day. I immediately started looking through my closet for the best outfit to wear. No, that looks too churchy and that's too short. Finally, I decided on a nice white blouse with a Peter Pan collar and a plaid, pleated skirt. My mother suggested I wear stockings and my Cuban heel shoes. I already planned to wear those shoes, but stockings? No way! I hate wearing stockings; none of them match my skin color, the closest color is Red Fox and they make my legs look like they don't belong to the rest of my body. Plus, I would have to wear a garter belt to hold them up. I hate garter belts too, because they never hold the stockings up on my little skinny legs; they either sag at the knees or wrap around my ankles, sometimes both they're a mess to wear! Somebody should invent stockings attached to panties so all you have to do is pull them up, maybe one day…

My mom made another suggestion; "You should wear a hat and white gloves too."

Really mom? That's a bit much; who walks around these days with a hat and white gloves on besides church girls? I'm not going to church. No way, am I wearing wear a hat or gloves; are you kidding me? The next day, I got up early, got dressed, and took the Number 42 bus into town. The telephone building was located downtown in Center City. It was a tall, silver, modern-looking building with lots of windows, and to get to it, you had to cross a big street called Parkway. The street had four lanes of traffic coming and going in opposite directions. It was like a symbolic moat you had to first cross in order to get to the "Land of Oz."

I waited patiently for the light to turn green before I stepped off the curb I looked left, than right. I got as far as the middle of the street when suddenly, the light changed and traffic started barreling toward me. I stopped dead in my tracks; I didn't know whether to keep going or run back.

Cars began honking at me to get out of the way; I quickly ran ahead and jumped up on the curb on the other side. Phew, that was a close call! I straightened my clothes and checked to make sure the clip-in bow I put on top of my flip hairdo was straight. Then I began to ascend up the long, wide steps and went through the shiny, glass revolving doors.

When I got inside, I quickly realized I wasn't the only one who saw the ad, because there were at least fifty other girls applying for the same job. I completed a long application; when I finished, I looked around and noticed I was the only black girl in the room. There was one light-skinned black woman sitting behind the receptionist desk, but all the applicants were white; including a bunch of Catholic school girls; I knew they were Catholic because they had on school uniforms with their school's name imprinted on them Little Flower West Catholic Girls and Hallahan were the few I noticed.

The receptionist gathered them all together and led them out of the room. Their uniforms seemed to give them an advantage; it also looked like they were getting special treatment. Another lady came in and took the rest of us to another room and told us take a seat. She announced we were going to take a test; I got a little nervous, because I was never a good test taker. She gave us all Number 2 lead pencils and instructed us to completely fill in the little circles on the test paper; then she handed out the tests. About an hour later, she came back in and said that time was up; she came by and collected the tests, one by one. Then she told us to go back to the room we were in previously and wait for further instructions.

I had to go to the bathroom, so I asked the receptionist if I could use the restroom. She handed me a key with a big piece of wood attached to it and told me to make sure to bring it back, then pointed me toward the bathroom. While I was in one of the stalls, a few of the Catholic school girls came in. They were all talking at the same time. I overheard one of them say that she knew she was going to get hired because her Ant worked for the telephone company and was going to make sure she got in. I thought, What's the point of going through this if all white girls have to do is have somebody on the inside look out for them? I'm usually a positive person, but at that point I began to feel a little down. The same thing keeps happening and the white girl always comes out on top. But I soon perked back up I have to stay positive.

I went back in the room and took a seat. While I was sitting there, I noticed my nails looked dirty, even though I had just washed them. The lead in the Number 2 lead pencil I used to take the test must have gotten underneath my nails, and they looked terrible. Then I remembered; right before I left the house, I noticed the white gloves my mom suggested I wear sitting on the table, so I grabbed them and threw them in my sling bag.

I opened my purse and put them on; that solved that problem. After a while, a different woman came out and called my name. When I stood up, she seemed a bit surprised; I could tell she wasn't expecting to see a black girl. She gave me a quick look over, and told me to follow her. She led me to a small cubicle, where she sat behind a desk and pointed for me to take a seat on the other side. She had my application and began reviewing it. My work experience was limited, so there wasn't much to ask me about that. Then she began asking me questions about my home life and what I liked to do. Without skipping a beat, I began telling her about my aspirations to become an actress and the different productions I had been in and how I liked to sing and entertain people. I went on and on before I noticed she was staring at me, so I immediately stopped and apologized.

She said, "No, don't stop. I'm enjoying listening to you." Then she said something that kind of threw me off "You don't sound like a colored girl at all."

Huh? I just looked at her, I didn't know how to respond, so I just said; "Thank you."

She stood up, handed me her business card, and told me she would be in touch with me. She extended her hand and I reached out and shook it with my gloved hand. "I like your gloves." Again I said thank you, but in the back of my mind, I was saying, Thanks, Mom. I turned to leave, just before I left the cubicle, I looked back at her; she was still standing there looking at me, and she had a slight smile on her face.

Several weeks passed and I was really starting to get bored. My mom made me babysit my little brother, and every day she laid out a bunch of chores for me to do. This same routine was getting old really fast. I was fussing at my brother for not eating his Spaghettio's when I noticed the mailman had thrown some mail through the mail slot, I picked it up and started rifling through the envelopes. Most of them were bills addressed to my parents, but then I noticed a white envelope addressed to me. It had a recognizable icon on it, a little blue bell in the upper left-hand corner with the words "Bell of Pennsylvania" next to it. I nervously opened the envelope, took out the letter, and began reading it.

Dear Miss Geraldine Davis, you have qualified for employment at Bell of Pennsylvania. Please report for work... and it had a date written in. That's next week? I said out loud! Hot diggety dog! I could hardly wait for my parents to get home so I could tell them I was finally gainfully employed. The radio was on and I heard Georgie Woods; my favorite disc jockey, announce "Check out James Brown's funky new single "Say It Loud, I'm Black and I'm Proud." I picked up my little brother and started dancing around the kitchen with him.

"Sing with me," I told him.

He started singing "Say it loud, I'm bad and I'm loud!"

I cracked up laughing! "You sure are, little brother, you sure are."

Ma Bell

Getting a job with the telephone company was a bigger deal than I initially thought. They didn't just hire anybody; not only did you have to pass a test, but you also had to have a certain look and speak a specific way. They didn't hire blacks very often, so I felt very blessed. I was hired as a long distance operator; in those days, you had to dial "0" and go through an operator to make a long distance call. It didn't take me long to learn all the complicated connections on the massive switchboards and memorize the many different state area codes. Most of the senior operators were white women; there were a few black women with seniority, but they still had less than the white women did and they all got the better work hours. I really loved the job, even though I had to work a lot of different shifts, because work schedules were based on seniority, and I was low man on the totem pole, so to speak. But that didn't matter to me what else did I have to do?

A few other young black girls were hired the same time I was and we all went through training together. We stuck together and tried to help each other learn the job as much as we could. Some of the black women who were there before us were helpful, but many of them seemed reluctant to get too friendly with us. I guess they didn't want to lose whatever favor they had with their white counterparts, so us "young girls," as they called us, were pretty much on our own. Several of the white women outwardly showed their resentment toward us our very presence seemed to annoy them.

At the start and end of a long distance connection, we had to push a big lever on a time clock that monitored the length of time for each call so the caller could be charged accordingly. The time clock sat between each position, and operators on either side had to share the same clock. They would wrap a tissue or handkerchief around the lever to avoid touching it with their bare hands after we had touched it. There were several other unspoken insults we just ignored, but when I began hearing the "N" word hurled our way every time we left the break room or passed by, I couldn't ignore it any longer.

I first reported the incident to a white supervisor, there were no black ones at the time, but she simply shrugged it off. She even had the nerve to tell me it was probably my imagination; I looked at her like she was crazy.

The insulting and racist incidents continued until I finally confronted one of the white women and we got into a loud screaming match. I was written up and suspended without pay for a whole week, which really pissed me off, because they did nothing to the white woman. When is this shit going to end? I can't believe after all we've been through from slavery to civil rights, and here we are, still having to deal with white bigots who refuse to accept the fact that black Americans are here to stay. Instead of telling us we need to get over it, whites need to get over it. If only my saying it would make it so.

The Rocking Eighties

Twenty years have passed; it's the eighties and I've held many different positions since starting with the company in the sixties. Climbing the corporate ladder was never my ultimate goal at least not in the traditional way. Rather than seek out positions that paid the most money, I focused on positions that offered the most flexibility. Fortunately, I was always able to find positions that gave me the opportunity to work within the corporate confines and still be able to do my own thing at the same time. I used my self-delegated authority to plan my work and work my plan. Friends and colleagues often marveled at my ability to make things happen. I still don't know how I was able to do many of the things I did. I served as a community relations representative during and sometimes after company time, often without pay but I benefitted in other ways. This was especially important to me, because at the time the company was in the process of building a huge computer center right smack in the heart of a black neighborhood.

In order to make room for it, hundreds of homes would have to be destroyed in a community that was already feeling encroached upon by nearby Temple University. Many black residents who had lived in their homes for generations would be displaced. Even though they would be compensated, they simply didn't want to move or have their neighborhoods destroyed and who could blame them? Throughout this unsavory process, I attended community meetings and watched as several passionate, politicians and community activists fiercely fought and advocated on behalf of their neighbors and constituents. State Representatives Dave Richardson and Roxanne Jones to name a few, loudly voiced their opposition to the building of the computer center and stood up to company and city officials. Despite months of protests, the low-income residents simply were no match for a major company and politicians who supported the company's efforts. The deck was stacked against them; laws that allow government and corporate entities the right to take private property for public or business use left the residents out-ruled and outnumbered but not because they didn't try. That experience taught me how blurred the lines become when business and politics come together. Even though it was my job to help the residents feel better about the situation, I felt as defeated as many of them. I couldn't just walk away; I had to do something; so I successfully campaigned with others for the company to provide funding for youth programs. Those programs continued to make a difference in young people's lives for years.

I later became an active member in an employee professional development organization primarily made up of African American and Latino employees. The organization was comprised of several local groups throughout the northeast region. Our group coordinated training programs and motivational sessions for members. All the local groups joined together at an annual conference held at different hotels around the region. The conferences provided invaluable information useful for both your professional and personal life. Many of the training sessions offered college credits as well. Company executives were invited to update attendees with information about the many changes that were taking place in the telecommunications industry at the time. The conferences also featured many nationally known speakers, including the late Alex Haley, Susan Taylor, James Earl Jones, several noted authors Dr. Claud Anderson, Dr. Frances Cress-Welsing, Dr. Robin Smith, Dr Ben Carson and others. Over the years, the conferences grew in popularity, particularly among African American employees and the attendance began to swell. At that time there was only one African American executive officer who supported the organization from its inception. Initially, many other company executives were also supportive of the organization even provided funding for the annual conferences. It wasn't until a few white employees began complaining that they felt excluded and created a major brouhaha; that's when company officials threatened to withdraw funding. While the conference was founded on serving the needs of minority employees any employee could join a local group and attend the annual conference if they chose to. Even after launching a company-wide membership campaign, encouraging all employees to get involved, few white employees joined any of the local organizations or attended the conferences. After losing not only financial support but support in general from the top down, the organization began to wither and die on the symbolic vine, and the conferences that had meant so much to so many eventually ended. "Another one bites the dust."

Miss Penny

I recently landed a new position, a very unique one. It didn't even have a title or job description when I started. I actually had to write my own job description and negotiate my own pay scale, because it was the only position of its kind. The department manager was a white woman named Penny Schultz. She was a tall, slender, bleached blonde with a Marilyn Monro-ish-type persona. Some found her attractive particularly men, but to me she looked like a loose floozy; just saying. She was married to an upper level executive in the company; rumor has it she stole him away from his former wife and judging from her flirtatious behavior particularly around men, the rumor may have some validity.

You could tell she was from the other side of the tracks so to speak by the way she dressed and spoke. She often bragged about her humble beginnings: the daughter of a milkman, growing up in a Philly neighborhood primarily inhabited by lower socio-economic eastern European immigrants. She would end her self-deprecating stories with, "But look at me now," as she stretched her arms out over her imaginary empire.

Pulleeeze!

Miss Penny headed the Department of Administrative Services and Executive Support. Her department managed the ancillary departments that supported the company: the mailroom, graphics, car pool, and other support groups. Her employees did everything from sorting company mail to scheduling reservations on the corporate jet, and other forms of first-class travel arrangements for company executives. She also coordinated all the board meetings, staff meetings, and executive meetings with officers from other major corporations; she would personally oversee these meetings and concentrated most of her attention on them. On board meeting days, she acted as if it she was debuting in a Broadway play. Miss Penny had a reputation for using her lofty position to force herself on anyone who might oppose her, for fear of her ties to the executives. When she walked through the halls, people would literally clear a path for her and her staff, of which I was now one. I must admit it was pretty heady at the time. Even though I didn't have a clear understanding of what my position might entail when I accepted the position, somehow I knew it would be a great opportunity to see as well as be seen in corporate headquarters.

Soon after becoming part of Miss Penny's unconventional entourage, I began to realize that she wasn't very smart. Her spelling was deplorable she covered up her misspellings by scribbling her writings, making it difficult to read; her grammar was that of a 5th grader and her sentence structure left much to be desired. Her basic lack of intellect was no secret many others realized it too, but no one dared say anything. It was public knowledge the only reason she had that job was because of her husband who many respected and didn't want to offend and the support of other white men she was able to charm with her looks and seductive manner. She had very few female allies; most of the white female managers would smile in her face, then talk behind her back. I quickly recognized that what she needed was a confidante, someone she felt would watch her back and make her look good perhaps someone like me; why not?

I have to give it to her for recognizing I was smart, savvy, and had a knack for organization and details; skills she was totally void of. But what she didn't know is that I recognized as a black woman in a white corporation, I could also use someone like her to further my own personal goals and aspirations. Almost by osmosis, we formed an unusual and unspoken alliance, one where she believed she had the upper hand I voluntarily gave her. Even though she told me many times to just call her Penny I preferred to call her "Miss Penny," because it fit her so well. To me, the "Miss" signified a plantation mistress in the antebellum south she reminded me of Scarlett O'Hara and continued to call her Miss Penny.

Initially, Miss Penny had me proofing, as she called it, her memos and letters she sent the executives, their secretaries, and replying to her e-mails, without saying she expected me to make any corrections before always sending them under her signature. It wasn't long before she had me doing all of her writings. Once, she even had me write a proposal for a sales event; the company announced they were having an internal contest for employees only. They were introducing new products and needed a good sales promotion. The winner of the contest would receive an all-expense paid five-night, four-day stay in Las Vegas. Hundreds of employees submitted suggestions for ads. Wouldn't you know it; the sales promotion I wrote and submitted under Miss Penny's name *won!* Everyone was amazed when it was announced she was the winner even she seemed stunned when she heard her name but she dramatically accepted all the credit and accolades as if she wrote it herself. Not even when we were alone did she ever acknowledge it was my work or thanked me. The promotion was later televised; she never told me, I heard she received a significant bonus for the work.

Most knew there was no way she could have thought of that promotional ad on her own and a few secretly told me so, but no one ever spoke up, including me. I chalked it up to experience. I associated with the main character in a novel I read years ago written by Sam Greenlee; *The Spook Who Sat by the Door* and began to take full advantage of my surreptitious position. Two can play at that game.

I was in and out of the executive offices often, and had a special ID badge I used to swipe in the elevator that allowed it to go up to the top floor, where the executives and their secretaries were located. One day as I was leaving the floor, I stopped to use the restroom next to the bank of elevators, which I had done many times before. While I was washing my hands, a new white secretary I had seen before but was never introduced to said to me "You shouldn't be in here." I pretended I didn't hear her, to be sure I heard her correctly I said "Excuse me?"

"There's a service bathroom in the back, you should use that one." The bathroom she was referring to was in fact one the housekeepers used, I had previously used it as well; it was no big deal to me. It took everything in me to maintain my composure, but I remained cool.

I calmly said to her "I'm well aware of that bathroom, but this one was closer, so I decided to use this one instead. Do you have a problem with that?"

She gave me an icy stare and left in a huff. As I waited for the elevator, I noticed her talking to one of the other secretaries who knew me very well; who began waving at me, but I ignored them both and got on the elevator. The next time that new secretary saw me she jumped up from her desk, fell over her trash can, and was frantically waving, trying to get my attention. I just nodded in her direction and kept going. As I passed her by, I couldn't help but snicker as she tried to remove her foot that had gotten stuck in her trash can. I just shook my head and thought; I'm so sick of these privileged white bitches thinking they own the world.

By this time, many of the executives knew me by name as well as my talent. Some of them began asking me for advice about special events and sales promotion activities, while others asked me if I would advise their wives on how to plan a dinner party. One of them came right out and asked me if I would plan a Fourth of July party at his home. Usually Miss Penny handled any outside events for the officers and their wives, often with me and a few of her inner staff tagging along to assist her. But this was the first time I was personally asked to coordinate an event exclusively. I wondered how this would go over with her. I thought it was best that I come right out and tell her before she heard it through the grapevine.

When I began telling her, she had her head down, shuffling papers around her desk, which she often did when she wanted to appear busy. But once I told her what I was asked to do, she immediately stopped and looked up; she stared at me for what seemed like a long time. Before saying; "Fine, if that's what they want" and immediately went back to shuffling papers.

I was somewhat surprised, I expected more push back from her; I didn't think she would take it so well. So with her knowledge and dubious support, I began planning a great event for the executive. I wasn't naïve though; I knew her all too well. I suspected she might have some resentment, so throughout my planning I continually asked her for input, just to appease her. It was all about playing a part and remaining in character; I learned how to do that back in high school. She freely provided me with advice and didn't show any outward behavior that would make me think she didn't have my best interest at heart, but I still didn't fully trust her.

The executive's home was located in a nearby Philadelphia suburb. It was beautiful and sat on a hillside with a gorgeous view; a perfect sight for the fireworks I had arranged for later that evening.

Everything went off without a hitch; the guests raved about the food, the decorations were beautiful, and the soul band I hired kept everyone on the dance floor; it was a fun party. As the party was in full bloom, I noticed Miss Penny across the floor and started walking toward her. I was curious what she thought of the party and also wanted to thank her for input, even though I didn't really need it. As I approached her, the executive's wife stepped right in front of me.

She gleefully said "Gerri, this is by far the best party I've ever had. I can't thank you enough. You did a wonderful job." She gave me a customary two-cheek, Hollywood air kiss.

I smiled and thanked her before she flitted off. I looked back to where Miss Penny had been standing, but she was gone. The time came for the fireworks to start, so I gathered everyone around. I had a walkie-talkie to communicate with the guys I hired to conduct the fireworks.

I instructed them to wait for my signal, but when I tried to make contact with them, I got no response. I continued to try to reach the lead guy. "Moe, come back. Come back, Moe." Everyone was looking at me as I kept trying to reach the fireworks guys, but I heard nothing. Somebody suggested I switch channels; I tried that, but still nothing. To be safe, I had the fireworks guys located a distance from the house. I apologized to the anxious guests and sent someone from my staff down the hill to alert them.

In the meantime, I kept trying to figure out what was going on with the walkie-talkies. My husband, who always attended my events to assist me where needed came up and took the walkie-talkie from me. He began looking it over, I heard him say;

"Look, no batteries, there are no batteries!"

"What?" How could that be? I said. "They were there a few minutes ago, I checked them myself.

Just then, the fireworks went off. Thank goodness! My assistant must've reached the guys and not a moment too soon. Everyone began cheering; I was so relieved. The fireworks were spectacular. I breathed a huge sigh of relief; as I turned to walk away I saw Miss Penny again and she was looking at me; she had a cynical smirk on her face that I couldn't quite read.

I went to her and said; "That was a close call". "Yes it was" she replied and then proceeded to say; "Well, like I always say, don't trust anyone you can't throw any further."

What the hell does that mean? What a bimbo! I thought to myself. I didn't give a damn what she thought; I had proven myself and that was all that mattered to me.

-I remained in that position for a few more years. I learned a lot about the inner workings of a major corporation and had made some great contacts along the way that would come in handy later. I also started my own special event management company and had numerous clients outside of the company. There were times when I was no longer available to work with Miss Penny on the weekends anymore, and she didn't like that, not at all.

Even though she paid me generously, the money didn't matter to me; I simply preferred to do my own thing. I was beginning to feel like my growth was being stymied, plus there were no similar internal positions I could transition to, or so I thought.

She had become even more insufferable and more demanding of my time. She never asked, and I never offered, but she learned about my outside activities, which seemed to make her even more intolerant. She often overheard people congratulate me for the many successful events I coordinated for companies like CIGNA Insurance, United Negro College Fund, and other major organizations. She started making little snide remarks to me in public trying to embarrass me, "You're not a real planner; don't forget girlie, I taught you everything you know."

Nothing could be further from the truth; before she met me, she didn't even know how to hold a fork and knife properly. I even taught her how to dress; bringing in outfits for her to try on from a friend's upscale boutique. I encouraged her to change her tawdry dress style to clothing more suitable to her professional status is how I approached her. I made an appointment and accompanied her to a chic hair and makeup salon where they advised her as I had many times before, that less was more. They managed to convince her to get rid of the stupid mole she drew on her face with a black Maybelline eyebrow pencil that was usually smeared by the end of each day. I had mentioned that to her as well many times before. I essentially gave her a total transformation. I certainly did far more for her than she ever did for me. Simply put, I outclassed her!

At the time, many corporations were undergoing major financial and social shifts and began restructuring and downsizing to save money. I immediately saw the writing on the wall and knew that non-income-producing departments like the one I was in would be first on the chopping block and started looking for another position. I didn't tell Miss Penny but she soon found out that I was applying for other positions and started trying to sabotage my move. She did subtle things at first, like refusing to give me a referral or not allow me to go on interviews. But when she realized I wasn't going to let her shenanigans stop me, she got serious and becme vindictive. One evening, I was working late on a project she gave me at the end of the day and wanted it completed in time for a meeting first thing the following morning. I needed to ship an overnight package to one of my outside clients, but I didn't have one my own imprinted FEDEX envelopes. It was the last pick up of the day, and I needed the package to go out that evening to ensure next-day delivery, so instead, I used a company FEDEX envelope from the mailroom. But before I mailed it, I scratched out the imprinted company ID number and return address and wrote my own information in its place.

The next day, I checked with my client to make sure it had arrived on time, which it did, and I didn't think anymore about it. Weeks later, I got a call from the company internal affairs department and was instructed to immediately report to a conference room. That made me a little nervous, because I couldn't imagine what they wanted to talk to me about. When I met with the agents, they proceeded to tell me they received a report that I was using company materials for my own personal use. I had no idea what they were talking about. Then they pulled out a copy of the FEDEX slip for the package I had mailed awhile back and asked me if I knew anything about it. Without any hesitation, I told them of course I did and went on to explain how and why I used the envelope. I even showed them my monthly credit card statement, which I had just received and ironically happened to have in my purse thinking that would resolve the issue and end the discussion. But they persisted; they still wouldn't accept what I was telling them, even with proof. They kept accusing me of stealing company funds and said it was cause for immediate dismissal. I was in shock! I couldn't believe they were accusing me of something so egregious. I continued to hold my position; there was no way I was going to let my decades of seniority and work experience go down the drain without a fight. I kept trying to explain to them over and over again why I did what I did and proved to them that there was no cost to the company. The interrogation went on for hours.

At one point, I tried to reach Miss Penny so she could vouch for me, but I couldn't reach her anywhere; I was on my own. As a black woman, I knew perfectly well that I was viewed with a different level of skepticism than a white woman would be I was used to that. After hours of going back and forth with the white investigators, who were clearly biased and refused to deal with the facts all of a sudden, they relented. Out of nowhere, they said "Okay, you can return to work." And just like that, it was over. No apologies, nothing. I couldn't believe it! After all they put me through, they simply dropped it. That's when I realized the whole thing was a setup from the very beginning to scare me, and quite frankly, it did. I still believe they would have fired me if they could have. I also came to realize just how easily your entire career could be destroyed and your reputation defamed by trumped-up charges made by someone others considered more credible than you simply because of their skin color; that's so wrong.

I never felt so helpless before in my entire life; I couldn't help but compare my situation with thousands of other innocent black and poor people who face similar circumstances with far more serious consequences. This was so unfair and terribly unjust I wanted to scream, but I felt no one would even hear me.

Miss Penny never mentioned the incident, she never even asked me where I had been all those hours while I was being interrogated, nothing, and I never said anything about it to her either. I was angry for a long time you can only hang on to anger for so long before it begins to affect you and she wasn't worth it. She'll get hers; *"Karma's a Bitch"* and what goes around, comes around, comes around. Even though Miss Penny refused to give me a referral, it didn't take me long to find another position, because my work ethic and reputation preceded me.

Once the word got out that I was seeking another position, several department heads offered me a job, even without me applying for it and in no time at all, I had a number of offers to choose from. Miss Penny had been giving me the cold shoulder for weeks, so I just stayed out of her way. When it was time for me to leave, I went to thank her for the opportunities I was afforded while I worked in her organization. I parsed my words carefully, so as not to give her much credit and keeping it short to avoid throwing up inside my mouth as I recited my empty departing statement. Without looking up from her desk, she gave me a phony, "Good luck" and went right back to shuffling papers like she always did. Even after leaving, I resented her for a long time before I finally let my festering anger go. My husband inadvertently helped me do that. After dinner one night, I found myself bitching again to him about all the things Miss Penny did to me. I guess he was fed up hearing about it and casually asked me; "What role did you play in all that"? What? What do mean, what role did I play? I was absolutely flabbergasted by his insensitivity, he knew better than anyone how much Miss Penny had put me through. But later, I thought about what he said, I recognized I did play a part; in a way we both had played each other and we both got what we deserved, DAMN! In the words of Oprah; "That was a AHA moment for me." I stopped letting Miss Penny rent space in my head without paying and evicted her. I was done with her, and apparently, I wasn't alone. Her husband recently retired, and people who had been tolerating her for years suddenly were no longer willing to put up with her crap! They all began closing ranks to get her out. They didn't have to wait long, because after a major company restructure, her department was totally eliminated, and she and her entire staff were included in a major reduction in force, but I'm sure she received an attractive severance package. That's how it often is, not only in corporate America, but life as well; corrupt, dishonest behavior often gets rewarded, and truthful, honest individuals get persecuted. Life ain't always fair; you just have to learn to roll with the punches.

Our paths never crossed again, but I heard her husband divorced her and went back to his former wife. I'm sure she'll land another unsuspecting man as well as another position of power; they're both one and the same as far as she was concerned. However, I couldn't shake a peculiar feeling like I had escaped from a plantation, Miss Penny's plantation. *Hmmm.*

The End

CHAPTER 5
Living Black in White Suburbia

I've been married for more than twenty years. My husband and I have four children; three sons and a daughter. He's a self-employed contractor with a successful new construction maintenance and high-rise window cleaning business. His company was the first minority owned and, for many years, the only company that specialized in the final cleaning of newly constructed sites in Philadelphia. Many of the high-rise structures dotting the Philadelphia skyline today were initially cleaned by his company. I'm very proud of my husband's business accomplishments.

I worked throughout all my pregnancies and took short maternity leaves with my first three children in order to maintain my seniority. After the birth of my fourth child, our financial status was much more stable, that, and the passage of the 1993 Family Leave Act allowed me to stay home with my children for a while, so I took a long leave of absence. However, I planned to return to work, because my mom always told me "God bless the child that has her own," and I hold to that tenet.

We had a beautiful home built in the suburbs of South Jersey, just a short commute from Philadelphia. Initially, moving to the suburbs came as a bit of a culture shock at least for me. My husband adjusted almost immediately, his first ride-on lawn mower was all he needed to seal his comfort level. Living in a predominantly white neighborhood was different and took some adjustment on my part. We were the only black family in our development at the time, but my children quickly made friends with the white children in the neighborhood. They played ball, rode bikes together and could even leave their bikes outside without fear of them being stolen; we all had to get accustomed to that. My husband built a large deck in our backyard with a barbecue pit; I often cooked out and fed my children and many of their new friends. Our home soon became a place where all the neighborhood kids hung out and that was fine with me, because it allowed me to keep an eye on my own children. Most of our neighbors were friendly, a few acted as if we were invisible and I was perfectly fine with that. Many of the parents came up and introduced themselves often by their first name and I did the same. It wasn't until their children began calling me by my first name too, that I became a bit bothered; I wasn't use to children addressing me by my first name. When it happened I would wait for the parents to correct them, but they never did. One of my children called one of the white mothers "Miss" she corrected him and said it was okay to call her by her first name, but I quickly spoke up and told her that was unacceptable. I let her know my children had to refer to adults by title: Miss, Mr., Mrs. something and I expected the same from other children. She didn't seem to comprehend, but her kids finally got the message after I corrected them a few times. Another thing I noticed when white parents called for their children, the children would respond by saying, "*What!* What?"

That was a no-no in my home; in most black households that I'm aware of. Black parents simply didn't allow their children to address them that way; it was seen as a sign of disrespect. My parents would have knocked me into the middle of next week if I said "What?" to them, and my kids knew better than to even try it. These were just a few nuances I noticed right off the bat. I grew up watching television programs like: Leave It to Beaver, Father Knows Best and the Donna Reid Show. I enjoyed those programs they shaped my beliefs and opinions of how white families lived, I didn't have anything else to go on. I never saw those behaviors acted out on TV but that was then and this is now. A lot has changed since then; black families have changed a lot too.

I'm not Having It!

We purposely planned our move over the summer so our kids could begin school at the start of the fall semester. The schools were primarily 98 percent lily-white the students, the teachers as well as the administrators. Coming from an all-black community, I wanted to make sure my children were prepared to deal with any slights or insults that might come their way particularly those related to the color of their skin. I didn't specifically talk about racism, instead I had a candid conversation with them about the "N" word and how they should handle themselves if it was ever said to them or around them. I was primarily speaking to my three older children, who were attending elementary, middle, and high school respectively. They seemed to care less about my cryptic talk, but I didn't care. I wanted to make sure they understood and were aware of what might happen. I told them under no circumstances were they to ever allow themselves to be called the "N" word by another student, whether white or black, and that included adults as well. If it ever happened, they were to speak up immediately. I even had them role-play a scenario with me where the "N" word was used in the lunchroom, I told them I wanted them to handle the situation right then and there. I emphatically said "The minute you hear that word, I want you to speak up, even if you have to slam your hand on the table to get everyone's attention and say, 'I'm not having it!'"

"Say it; I had each one of them repeat what I said, which they all did reluctantly.

"I'm not having it!" even the baby tried to say it and we all laughed. Good!

"Then come home, let me and Daddy know what happened, and we'll take it from there. Understand me?"

"Yes," they responded.

I knew most likely I would be the one handling it if the situation ever arose, my easy-going husband just wanted to go along to get along. After I felt satisfied they understood what I expected of them, I let the issue go. I later learned that my youngest son was more impacted by my talk than my older children. When he turned four, I enrolled him in pre-school before I returned to work. He was doing fine for a while until one day when his teacher called to tell me he was hitting the children, slamming his hand on the desk, and screaming something at them she couldn't quite make out. That was so unlike him he was usually a very kind and friendly child. When I picked him up, I asked him in front of his teacher why he was hitting and screaming at his classmates.

He calmly said to me "I don't like the letter 'N' and *I not habing it!"*

"What?" I asked him. That's when I realized he had associated the letter "N" with kids whose names began with "N," like Norman, Nicholas, Nyle, and Noelle. Through no fault of their own, those particular kids become an object of my son's innocent wrath, and he wasn't having it! I sheepishly apologized to his teacher, who had a perplexed look on her face. I needed to have another conversation with my Sesame Street-educated young son obviously one less radical.

Even though the residents in the South Jersey suburban community we lived in were predominately white, there were a good number of other upwardly mobile black families living throughout the township, and their children attended the same schools as ours. As a result, our children became friends consequently, many of the parents became friends too. The mothers bonded while picking up our kids from school or dropping them off at each other's homes for play dates, birthdays, and swim parties. When we were together, we began to discuss different concerns we all were beginning to have with the school system. The apparent lack of African American teachers was troublesome, but even more disturbing was that a number of our boys had been classified as ADD or ADHD and assigned to special education classes before we were even notified and without our sons being formally tested. This was a serious problem. Not only would this inhibit our children's academic advancement it also could have an affect on their self-esteem.

My eldest son was one of the boys targeted and as a ninth grader this issue was never brought to my attention before, so I couldn't help but wonder, Why now? What's different?

He was also a star athlete; several of the other black boys were athletes too. Ultimately, earning their teams multiple championships, particularly the high school, yet they were not eligible for scholarships and that was a problem. Education always came first in our household, my son's athletic ability was not as important as his education was to us. My husband and I and other black parents had met with school administrators individually to discuss our concerns, but to no avail. Most of us were professionals: doctors, attorneys, teachers, business owners, and corporate employees. We were all becoming frustrated about the troubling situation and decided to combine our efforts to better represent our common issues. We formed an advocacy group we named Coalition of Black Citizens or CBC. We hired a host of professional therapists to assess our children. After weeks of study, they found no indication of learning disabilities in any of them. We presented our findings to the school board with charts and scientific studies that revealed how black boys were often misdiagnosed with learning disabilities. After some time, as well as the threat of legal action, our sons were eventually allowed back into regular classrooms, and the surge of black boys assigned to special education classes miraculously stopped. Go figure!

The Prom

No sooner had that situation been resolved, another one suddenly cropped up; one I personally felt required our immediate attention too, but I soon found myself alone. The school district had recently issued a new rule that no students outside of the district were allowed to attend the prom. With a limited number of black students, particularly black boys, many of the black girls would either have to go to the prom stag or not attend at all. The white boys weren't asking black girls to the prom, but several of the black boys had asked white girls. That issue really hit home for me, because my son had also asked a white girl to attend his junior prom, and I had a real problem with that. I remembered how important my prom was to me, and I didn't want to see any girls, black or white, miss their prom for reasons that were beyond their control. I also found out many of the black parents whose sons had asked white girls to the prom didn't think it was a big deal, even those with daughters and that really surprised me. I tried to explain to my son how unfair the rule was to the many lovely black girls who would be left without dates. I always encouraged my children to speak their minds, so I patiently listened as my son adamantly stated his position. Both he and my husband felt he had the right to choose who he wanted to go to the prom with, I found myself outnumbered even in my own home.

This became a major point of contention in our household. My son and I went back and forth for weeks trying to convince the other. But at the end of the day, my parental role superseded my son's limited life experiences. I finally put my foot down and told him "If you can't ask 'Hattie' to the prom I absolutely forbid you from taking 'Heidi.'" It may have been a tacky metaphor, but he clearly understood what I meant. He wasn't at all happy with my firm position and decided not to attend the prom at all, and that was okay with me too. Many of my black friends accused me of not having an open mind or for not keeping up with the changing times. I was appalled by their dismissive attitudes and total disregard of our history. "Imagine if one of our sons was in a car with a white girl and stopped by some racist cop. Just think what could happen then? This is not just about the prom!"; I exclaimed. It's about fairness and doing what's best for our children. I remained steadfast, but alone in my position. I wrote several letters and attended school board meetings voicing my concerns. Surprisingly, a few white mothers started coming around to agree with me that the ruling was discriminatory, given the disproportianate ratio of black male students versus white male students. The following year, the school board lifted the rule. By that time, my son was a senior, and without any prompting from me he asked a black girl from another school to attend his senior prom. I felt vindicated!

Not because she was black though I admit it pleased me. Most importantly, I knew he finally understood that the ruling was simply unfair, which was my main objective all along.

The Coalition of Black Citizens became a force to be reckoned with. Not only did we introduce Black History month programs into the schools, we encouraged other ethnic groups to share their own respective holidays and celebrations: Cinco De Mayo, Chanukah, Chinese New Year, Hindu, and other celebrations. The diverse programs provided all students an opportunity to learn about other cultures and proved to be a win-win for all. We also were responsible for the hiring of black teachers and eventually a few black officers were added to the township police force, we believe, as a result of our continued advocacy of the need for diversity. The township even awarded the organization an "Excellence in Diversity" citation.

Over time, our community became more diverse and so did the growing number of other civic and social organizations. One in particular comprised of females from all backgrounds and ethnicities: white, black, asian, indian, african, latino, and more. The multicultural female organization instituted a program in the school system encouraging girls to take more STEM courses: science, technology, engineering and math. You go, girls!

"Oh No She Did-ent"

Many of the black mothers formed a tight circle of friends; we lunched, shopped together, and held a regular "Girls' Night Out" at each others' homes. We would leave our kids with our husbands or sitters and get together for some adult fun. One of the mothers in our group was white; she was married to a black man who was a professional athlete and asked to join our group, and we welcomed her. Several of the black wives were also married to professional athletes, so she was no exception. It was my turn to host the Girls' Night Out at my house. I planned a pajama party and told the girls to wear pajamas, which they all did. We were just going to hang out, eat, drink, gossip talk about our men, kids, sex, each other, and just have a lot of fun. The white girl in our group had worn a short baby doll pajama set, which I thought was inappropriate, but I didn't say anything; I figured to each her own. We were having fun playing a game of charades when I noticed the white girl wasn't wearing panties and she was sitting on my couch.

I blurted out; "Girl, you don't have any drawers on?"

She unabashedly smiled, and said "No, why?"

I thought for a second before I responded, I'm all for being free to be you and me, but this was a bit much. Then I said; "Why? Because my kids and husband sit on that couch; that's why. Are you crazy? You better get your naked, trifling ass off my couch; right now!"

The others girls began laughing, but I was dead serious. The next day, the white girl called me very upset she told me I had embarrassed her and felt I owed her an apology, which I absolutely had no intention of giving her. I told her she should have known better; who does that?

She explained, since we were all females, she didn't see what the problem was plus she didn't sleep in panties anyway.

"Who the hell cares?" I asked her. I let her know that was her personal business, and besides she wasn't coming for a sleepover, even if she was, no one needed to be exposed to her *va-jay-jay;* we all have one of our own thank you very much! She didn't agree with me and I certainly didn't agree with her, and simply agreed to disagree. Though we remained cordial when we ran into each other; I never invited her back to my home.

Growing up, my mother instilled in me a strict code of ethics and sensibilities. There were times I wasn't even allowed out the house without a slip on, much less underwear. That was simply unheard of.

I must admit, I always envied the freedom of movement white girls appeared to have: the way they were able to jump in a pool or walk in the rain with no concern about their hair; it looked so liberating. Just being able to take an "impromptu" shower with my husband takes some planning and careful maneuvering. There's also the way white girls often sat in public with their legs curled under them or crossed at the knees their upper thighs showing. My mom taught me young ladies sat with their legs crossed at the ankles. Back then, black mothers were particularly sensitive about how their girls might be perceived by others; it was their way of protecting us. That's just how I was raised. She may have been oldfashioned, but her lessons have served me well and I passed them on to my daughter, and I'm sure she'll do the same with her daughter.

Living and raising my family in the suburbs proved to be a great experience in understanding how other races live and raise their children. My children benefited as well; they learned early on how to get along with people from other cultures and backgrounds. I've built lifelong relationships with white women as well as women of other ethnicities and found, when given the opportunity to communicate and get to know each better, we can often find value in our differences and realize we have just as many similarities.

The End

CHAPTER 6
Retirement Interrupted

After thirty years of employment, I decided to retire from the telephone company. I've enjoyed every decade, every experience, the good and not so good, and the many unique opportunities I had has made me a better person and made my life so much fuller. It was a great company to work for, and I wouldn't change a thing.

My kids are grown now, well educated, and most importantly on their own. My free time didn't last long though, because my daughter announced her engagement soon after I retired. Having coordinated weddings for so many others for years, I now got to plan my own daughter's wedding, and I was really excited. Planning the engagement party, choosing a gown, the venue, the cake, DJ, photographer, videographer, it was a real whirlwind, but it was all worth it, because the wedding was absolutely fabulous! It wasn't long before she and my son-in-law announced they were expecting. That was the best news ever! I'm going to be a grandmom! It gets better; they were expecting twins, a boy and a girl. What a blessing!

Then out of nowhere amidst all that joy, I get diagnosed with breast cancer. My first reaction was I don't have time for this. Unfortunately, cancer doesn't care if you have time for it or not, because the clock starts ticking. You're immediately thrown into a morass of decision-making: lumpectomy, mastectomy, radiation, chemotherapy; it was overwhelming! I had a life to live, so this cancer crap had to get the hell out of me and fast! I decided to have a bilateral mastectomy with radiation. The surgery went off without a hitch, thank God but the healing process was horrible. While I was still recovering my temperature suddenly spiked and my right arm swelled up. I later learned I had a condition called lymph edema and it was permanent. What else, Lord? What else? But I refused to lie down and be run over by this unwanted and menacing condition. I had two bundles of joy coming into the world, and nothing, not even cancer was going to steal my joy away. The doctor cautioned me to not pick up anything heavier than twenty-five pounds or risk more swelling. But when those magnificent babies arrived at six and a half pounds each without hesitation, I picked up my babies and laid them in the pillow of my big arm and thanked God for the two angels he sent me to love forever and for the extra room he gave me to hold them.

For the next five years of my retirement, I babysat my beautiful twin grandbabies while my daughter worked and finished graduate school, which by the way she did all through her pregnancy. Baby sitting my grandbabies every day was the best time of my life. I actually find being a grandmother even more gratifying than I did raising my own children; who knew? Watching your grandchildren grow into healthy, fully developed young people really makes you appreciate and value the importance of family. I am truly blessed!

Time to give back

I've met many great women over the years and developed a close circle of girlfriends; I call them sister friends and I love them immensely. Some of our relationships go as far back as high school; many of us started at the telephone company at the same time and retired around the same time as well. My sister friends and I have been through a lot together: sickness, death, wealth, poverty, separation, divorce, grandchildren, aging parents, and everything else that life throws at you, and we're all still standing strong. There's nothing I enjoy more than being with my true sister friends. I'm closer to many of them than I am some of my own family members. As the saying goes "You can't choose your family, but you can choose your friends" and that's so true. My sister friends keep it real with me and they keep me balanced. I've benefitted from many women who willingly shared their knowledge and experience with me, and now I want to do the same for others.

I recently joined an organization of professional women who mentor young women in corporate positions. I find today's young women absolutely amazing. Their first generation technical knowledge gives them an innate ability to adapt to the ever-changing technologies that exist today. I marvel at how easily they manage to navigate the maze of new software, social media, and the like. Quite frankly I find the constant changes dizzying at times, but not them. The more gadgets and apps that come on the market, they grab them up and quickly incorporate them into their daily lives. That's why I surround myself with vibrant young women ascending on corporations at a phenomenal rate and bringing with them a host of new talents and skills that were unthinkable when I first started. I often tell them I learn more from them than I could ever teach them; fortunately, they keep me around anyway. Since joining the women's network, I've sat in on a series of dialogue sessions with tough subjects that they themselves selected. They run the gamut from "How to manage your career without losing yourself" to "Finding a man that's not intimidated by your higher salary or level of education"; both situations can be quite challenging. They never shy away from tough subjects that sometime make me squirm in my seat a little. These outspoken young women have no problem leaning in and speaking out, and I find their in-your-face personalities refreshing.

Tanesha and Marjorie

In the two years I've been involved in the mentoring group, I've met several delightful young women, but there are two in particular who I've become especially close to Tanesha and Marjorie. Tanesha Brown is a black, twenty-eight-year-old sales executive with a large pharmaceutical company. She attended Syracuse University for her undergraduate studies and has an MBA from Cornell University. She was raised by a single mother with four younger siblings in North Philadelphia; a low-income, inner-city community. Even with scholarships, she struggled to pay her way through school, and she's still paying off student loans. She worked hard to establish herself as a reputable powerhouse, both in her workplace as well as in her community. People easily gravitate toward her because of her energetic persona. Tanesha never forgot where she came from. She formed an organization for young black, white, and Latino girls from the same community she grew up in. The group promotes self-esteem and female empowerment. Each year, she hosts an annual awards banquet that includes a fashion show. She purchases clothes for the girls to model with donations she collects from friends and colleagues and contributes much of her own money. The girls show off their singing, dancing, and spoken word talents. I attended one of her banquets, and it was wonderful. She reminds me so much of myself when I was her age except for her academic achievements, which I sometimes regret not going back to attain. I know it's never too late.

Marjorie Dilworth, also twenty-eight, is white. She has a bachelor's degree from the University of Pennsylvania and is an executive with a major cable company. She was raised with both parents on the Main Line an affluent suburban community near Philadelphia. Her tuition was paid for by a trust fund that was set up by her grandparents when she was young; she has no student debt. Her family has a long, rich political history in Philadelphia, which provides her with some major connections, both political and business. Marjorie lights up a room when she walks in and makes everyone feel comfortable in her presence. Despite her advantages, she regularly works with those less fortunate than herself. She collects clothing from her affluent friends and donates them to a career wardrobe agency for low-income women seeking employment. She also conducts mock interviews with the women to help them hone their interviewing skills.

Both Marjorie and Tanesha actually have a lot in common. They're both attractive, sophisticated young women who are serious about their career paths, yet conscientious enough to give back and take time to support others; I find their commitment admirable. They each belong to different chapters of the mentoring organization; Tanesha belongs to the city chapter and Marjorie the suburban one and I go between both, so they don't know each other, but I plan to introduce them to each other as soon as the opportunity presents itself. They're also both single, and like many other women their age they're seeking relationships that will hopefully lead to marriage. They don't shy away from their desires to be married and have children, and both talk about feeling the ticking of the biological clock. However, judging from the sordid stories they've both told me, neither one of them have had much luck in the dating game. I find that quite surprising, given all the social media outlets they're connected to: Facebook, Linkedin, Twitter, Instagram not to mention the numerous dating Web sites they're constantly checking in on, and in addition, they both blog. I'm exhausted just thinking about their active social lives. Ironically, they both told me about a new guy they met online, and they each seem to hit it off with their respective mates; I wished them both well. Tanesha and Marjorie are exceptional young women and they both deserve a good, loving and healthy relationship.

One day, I was having coffee with Marjorie after one of our group meetings. She kept going on about a guy she recently met on-line. I'm still amazed by how these girls meet guys on-line, date and if it works fine, if not they simply move on. She was gushing on excitedly; telling me even though they had only been dating for short period of time, he excited her in a way no other man ever had.

"Well, that's a lot of excitement!" I told her.

She also shyly admitted to sleeping with him on their first date, which she said she never did before, but he was so desirable she couldn't help herself. According to her, their feelings were mutual and neither one of them could keep their hands off the other. She even told me about a birthday gift she had given him; an expensive red cashmere sweater.

What? ; I asked her. "C'mon, Marjorie, I can't believe you're buying this guy gifts already."

To my surprise, she replied; "It was his birthday and we're dating; I had to give him something."

I was incredulous! I just looked at her, wondering how someone so smart could also be so naïve at the same time. I cautioned her to slow down; and find out more about the guy, learn about his family, his lifestyle as much as she could. But I could tell she wasn't listening to anything I had to say, she was too far gone. However, she did tell me she appreciated my concern and knew what she was doing. She told me matter-of-factly she believed in love at first sight and felt he was the man of her dreams and wasn't about to let him slip away. I could see how serious she was; I didn't want it to become an issue between us and risk damaging our relationship, so I just dropped the subject and hoped she really did know what she was doing.

Mr. Casanova

After one of our city chapter meetings, Tanesha offered me a ride to the train station. I don't drive in town often, because the traffic is always crazy and the parking fees are synonymous to paying a car note. I took her up on her offer; it would give us a chance to catch up. As she was driving, she began telling me about a guy she had also met online. What's up with all this on-line dating? I thought to myself. She said; "First of all, he's *fo-wine*" that's a word young black women use to emphasize a man's super good looks "He's charismatic, dresses well and smooth as silk, again, her words. As she was talking, I kept looking at her. Tanesha's usually rather somber, I wasn't used to seeing her show so much excitement. Apparently, This guy clearly had made an impact on her. She went on to say; he was educated, had a good job, and checked off all the things on her long list of *he has to haves*. While she was telling me about him, her phone rang, and suddenly a man popped up on her cell phone mounted on her dashboard. Before answering she mouthed to me, whispering as she pointed "That's him."

She pushed the speaker button and continued driving. "Hey, Boo, what you up to?" I heard him say "Oh, you're a poet now, huh?"; they both laughed. He had a nice deep voice. I kept trying to avert my eyes away and looking out the window to give her some privacy. But I was curious what the guy looked like, so I took a quick glance at her phone screen. She was right; he is "*fo-wine*"! He had chocolate brown skin, chiseled features, a dimpled chin, and straight, white teeth. She complimented him on the red sweater he was wearing; he thanked her saying it was a belated birthday gift.

She said "Nice." They continued talking for a few minutes and made plans to meet later that evening. After she hung up, she had a cheesy smile plastered across her face.

I couldn't help it and asked her "My, my, my; you're really into this guy, aren't you?"

"I am," she admitted sheepishly; "I never met a guy like him before. He's spiritual, family-oriented; we have great conversations and like many of the same things. I think he might be the one, Ms. Gerri."

"Really? is that so?" I asked her. "Well, pump your brakes a bit; get to know him a little better." Basically, the same thing I told Marjorie.

Judging, from the dreamy look on her face, I could see she was in a world of her own and my words didn't mean a thing to her.

I talked to both Tanesha and Marjorie as if they were my own daughters. I encouraged them to not settle for what feels good at the moment, because that was fleeting and to not just look at the outside of a man; instead focus on what's in his heart and his soul. Take time to find out if he's a good person, that he has principles and shares the same values as you. Most of all, make sure he likes you; never mind whether or not he loves you. That will come later if it's meant to be.

Weeks passed and I was frantically trying to keep up with my hectic schedule. I had two major events coming up; and they were both scheduled on the same day at approximately the same time; a large one and a smaller one, and I really needed help. I asked Tanesha and Marjorie if they could give me a hand, and fortunately, they both agreed. I was relieved not only for their assistance, but I would finally have a chance to introduce them to each other. I decided to have them both work on the large event together that way, I could concentrate all of my attention on the smaller one. Part of the large event included a fashion show. Tanesha had lots of experience coordinating fashion shows, so choosing her to manage that project was a no-brainer. She was excited and I had no doubt she would do a great job. Marjorie is a people person and a great multitasker; both attributes made her a perfect match for managing the registration process, and she got right on it. She came up with a program that enabled registrants to print their registrations online and skip the check-in process when they arrived. What a whiz! I was so impressed.

The day came for both events. I had introduced them to each other weeks before at a planning meeting, and they hit it off right away, just like I knew they would. I also had given them their assignments previously; I just needed to stop by and brief them on all the arrangements before I had to leave for my other event. I felt comfortable leaving this event in both their capable hands. I thanked them, hugged them both, and hurried off. As I was leaving, I noticed a handsome, young man walking toward me.

Hmmm, I thought to myself. *He sure has some sexy bow legs.* He also looked familiar, but I couldn't recall where I knew him from. As he got closer, it came to me. That's Mr. Casanova, Tanesha's friend! The same guy I saw pop up on her cell phone; he even had on the same red sweater she complimented him on that day. I was just about to pass by him by, when surprisingly, he stopped me. At first, I assumed he knew me not that I knew how, because we had never met; that I could remember anyway.

I smiled at him and said hi.

He casually replied; "Excuse me, do you know where I can find Marjorie?"

Immediately, I was taken aback; why was he asking for Marjorie? Maybe he said Tanesha and I thought I heard him say Marjorie. So I asked him; "I'm sorry, who?"

"Marjorie; Do you know her and where I can find her?"

Now, I was completely baffled; I couldn't even respond to him. I just stood there staring at him, like a fool. I almost asked him if he meant Tanesha, but I stopped myself. My mind was racing trying to figure out what to do and what to say; I know I needed to do something, but I didn't know what to do. I was still pondering what to say to him, apparently, the handsome young man got tired of waiting and started to walk away, but I grabbed his arm. I was still mulling things over in my head when I felt something tugging at me. That's when I realized I was still holding the young man's arm, and he was trying to pull away from me. I apologized, but continued to hold onto him. I curved my arm into his and offered to escort him to Marjorie. I was trying to delay him as long as I could, while at the same time trying to figure out what was going on. Could this man be the same person they were both dating at the same time? Nooo! Impossible! That just couldn't be; could it? As I was walking with him, I began to make small talk. I had just introduced myself and was about to ask him how he knew Marjorie, when a voice we both recognized came from behind us.

"What are you doing here?"

Damn! It was Tanesha! We both turned around at the same time. Tanesha was standing there looking confused; trying to figure out why her man was there and probably why the hell he was arm in arm with me. Marjorie was just feet away at the registration table she looked up to see where all the commotion was coming from. At first, she smiled when she saw her man, but her smile slowly began to fade.

Mr. Casanova just stood there frozen in place, like a deer in headlights. Both Tanesha and Marjorie had looks of absolute disbelief on their faces. I felt so helpless. I stepped aside, realizing something bad was about to happen, something really bad something no one could have ever imagined or planned for. Two universes were about to collide.

Epilogue

"Since the beginning of mankind, men have attempted to control a woman's sexuality. At times women have used their sexuality to get what they needed or wanted. Today, this dichotomy often distracts women from empowering themselves and redirecting their energies to develop their own God-given superior strengths."

The End

"We are more alike, my friends, than we are unalike."
Maya Angelou
-Rest in Peace-